VENTURE CAPITALIST

Book 3

Desire

Venture Capitalist: Desire/Ainsley St Claire—1st edition

Ainsley St Claire

VENTURE CAPITALIST

Book 3

Desire

A Novel

chapter ONE

HADLEE

LOOKING AT MY REFLECTION in the mirror, I can't believe I chose this bridesmaid dress. Emerson asked us to pick the same color and fabric—we went with black silk and organza—but she wanted us all to choose a dress style that complements us.

Doing a quick spin in front of the mirror, all I see are my breasts. Reaching into the bodice, I adjust both of them. I say with disgust, "I'm thirty-two years old, and I swear my tits are still growing. Fuck!" I'm pouring out of this dress. It's almost pornographic.

Jesus! I'm a pediatrician, for God's sake, not a porn star.

At least for a change, with the help of a firm pair of Spanx, I have a nice, trim waist. My dress is a lushly gathered organza full-length halter gown with a high slit to show off some leg. I loved it when I was with the seamstress. Now, not so much. I would hate to find one of these monster tits making an unexpected entrance during the wedding or reception.

With a light spritz of perfume, I check my makeup one last time and take a closer inspection. I'm taped in, and this as good as it's going to get. Ready as I'll ever be, I walk out of my room, and I have a bit of spring to my step. I'm off to the hotel lobby to meet the rest of the wedding party.

My good friend, Emerson, and her soon-to-be husband, Dillon, are getting married today, and I'm a bridesmaid. It's so exciting to be here this weekend. I'm the only one in the wedding party who isn't a family member, a partner, or an advisor to SHN. Emerson and Dillon really give a single girl like me hope that there's a happily ever after for smart, strong, and capable women. San Francisco's a tough place to meet many single, straight men.

I spot Sara and her new fiancé, Trey, who also happens to be my best friend's brother. They look sharp standing together. Sara's stunning with her hair wrapped up in a French twist, and her neck brilliantly sets off the Mikimoto pearl choker and matching earrings that Emerson surprised us each with last night as our wedding party gift and for us to wear for the wedding.

Trey's always handsome with his piercing blue eyes and chocolate-brown hair that's slicked back to keep his curls at bay. I'm watching the groomsmen arrive, and they're all dressed in black tuxedoes with white shirts. Dillon gave his groomsmen beautiful white-gold Mikimoto pearl cufflinks. These handsome men take my breath away. They could easily pass for models instead of high-powered venture capitalists and billionaires.

I look at Sara and Trey. Sara greets me with a big hug. "That dress puts mine to shame. Wow!"

Blushing, I lean in and say, "The girls keep trying to escape."

"Lucky Cameron," Sara whispers and winks at me. She knows I have a crush on my escort for the evening. But despite the pairing, he's never even flirted with me, so I don't think I'm his type. Plus, I brought my current boyfriend. I'm determined to have fun at this wedding.

Fuck Cameron.

Trying to be inconspicuous, I gaze around until I spot him. My stomach drops to the floor like a fish out of water. Typically, Cameron wears jeans, a pair of trendy sneakers, a concert T-shirt, and a baseball cap. Today his dirty blond hair is slicked back, thick and lustrous. His eyes are a mesmerizing deep brown that are so dark, they almost seem black with flecks of gold. His face is strong and defined, his features molded from granite, and his dark eyebrows that sloped downward always give him a serious expression. His usually playful smirk is drawn into a hard line across his face, his perfect lips ripe for the kissing.

I sigh for what will never be, then can't help but blush. "Shh. Here he comes."

His voice is deep, with a serious tone. His arms wide as I step in for a cordial hug, his lips brush my ear as he speaks. "Hadlee, you are even more beautiful than usual."

His fingertips touch my bare back, and an audible gasp escapes my dry lips. *Oh God, how embarrassing. Maybe I can play it off as if it's a sore throat.* Thankfully he didn't seem to catch my gasp, and I take in his smell. It is positively divine—spicy ginger with a hint of citrus. Very distracting.

You'd never guess that I grew up as part of the 1 percent. These days I live an average life as a pediatrician working with the San Francisco poor. You'd think with all my education, I wouldn't be so nervous about being close to Cameron, but I've never met anyone who made my mouth go dry or my stomach drop like he does.

Quickly Siobhan, Dillon's sister, arrives with her dress that resembles something Audrey Hepburn would've had in her closet. And right behind her are Greer and CeCe.

I hug them both and turn to Greer. "You look beautiful." She twirls around, the short dress showing off her long legs.

Greer admires my dress and shares, "What I wouldn't give to have a chest like yours. This dress only works if you have fried eggs for tits."

"Get over yourself. You're both perfect," CeCe bemoans. CeCe's dress is something to behold as well. She showed it to me before we left for the Colorado destination wedding. "Wow! Ce, your dress turned out fantastic. You both look stunning."

As we wait, we gossip about last night's rehearsal dinner. We were given a very strict schedule by the wedding planner with a proverbial death threat if we're late. Now we're waiting for a car service to transport us to the first half of the wedding photos.

I hear Tina, the wedding planner, before I see her. "We seem to have the wedding party all here," she whispers into headset, and a stretch Cadillac Escalade pulls up to the hotel lobby. It's a tight fit for the ten of us, but we all manage to climb in after a couple minutes.

We're driven to a small park above Lake Dillon, where we meet the wedding photographer who has Dillon with her for our pictures. I stop and stand still a moment, taking in the view. I grew up in San Francisco and have been to Colorado before, but usually during ski season. It's fall now, and the weather is crisp but not too cold. Under blue and sunlit skies, the view's wondrous to behold. In a valley at the foot of the Rockies, the lake teems with life—early boaters and swimmers. The mountains are covered with a rug of pine trees and the yellow rivers of the changing aspens, but their bare mountaintops are ensconced with a light snow that fell last night. "Wow. This is stunning. The mountains and the lake are majestic."

Two hours later, we've been posed together, apart, in pairs, and carefully with the groom. Dillon's white as a sheet, though I can't be sure if the guys got him drunk last night and he's hung over, or if it's just nerves.

When it's my turn to pose with Dillon, I lean over and ask, "How ya feelin'? Do you think you might like a Valium? You're either having an anxiety attack or you're hung over."

He looks at me, astonished, and then a smile crosses his face as he visibly relaxes. "No, maybe a little nervous."

"Well, I know I typically treat anxiety in children, but I can tell you're getting a little stressed. I'm afraid you're cutting the blood flow off to your extremities. I get it, you're going to be stuck with one of my best friends for the rest of her life, but you should be enjoying this."

He puts his arms around me. "I'm so glad you're here. And glad to know you can get me Valium if I ever need it. Cameron must be going crazy with you in that dress."

I'm shocked over this, considering Cameron, much to my disappointment, has never looked twice at me. "First, Cameron doesn't like me like that, and second, I only asked if you might like a Valium. I can only write prescriptions for my patients, and unless you age backward, you're too old for me."

Leaning in and whispering so only I can hear, he shares, "I think Cameron's a fool if he doesn't like you like that. But I wonder... could you give the wedding planner a little dose of a Valium? Maybe she'd relax a minute."

"She is wound a bit tight."

"That's a lot nicer way of putting it than what I was thinking."

The photographer has all of the bridesmaids surrounding Dillon and is posing us with Tina's help. She may be five foot nothing in her heels, but she commands a lot of attention.

When we finally finish, Tina marches us back to the waiting car and loads us up again to head to the church so we can meet up with the bride. After driving into Breckenridge to St. Mary's Catholic Church, the bridesmaids are shown to the vestibule, and the men are left with a member of Tina's team to get their job assignments.

Emerson's standing with her mother and one of her brother's wives. She's a vision of beauty. I walk over to her, taking in the contrast of sheer lace and the smooth, lustrous silk. It's quintessentially Emerson—elegant and romantic from the front. CeCe asks her to twirl around, and it shows off the deeply cut back, which gives it a spine-tingling sexy finish.

We circle around Emerson. "Wow. You make a beautiful bride."

Emerson reaches out and hugs each of us. "You all look beautiful. Thank you so much for coming and sharing this with Dillon and me."

I ask, "Are you nervous at all?"

"Of course. We have many more people here than we expected, and these heels?" Emerson holds up her dress and shows off her beautiful white satin stiletto sandals. "I'm more concerned about falling flat on my face in front of everyone."

"You are going to be fine," CeCe assures her. "And we'd better warn Mason that Dillon will have a huge hard-on when he sees you. He should be prepared to stand in front of Dillon to shield him if needed."

We all laugh, but we also know she's absolutely right. Emerson is positively stunning.

As we gossip over how handsome the groomsmen look, a member of Tina's team walks up and introduces herself. "Hi, I'm Valerie. I'll be working with you ladies. We have forty minutes until we walk down the aisle. There're some snacks over there." She points to a table at the side of the room with water, juices, fruit, and some light snacks. "Please help yourself."

I would love to eat my way through the snack table. Cheese and crackers look yummy. You can keep the carrots and celery sticks. I'm sure my stomach is growling but it'll only be a few more hours, and then I can get out of this dress and gain back the ten pounds I lost to wear it.

CeCe's shown how to button up Emerson's train, and we all visit while we wait. We hear the music begin, a classical piece starts playing over the speakers and Valerie announces, "Guests have begun arriving."

I wonder if I need to ask Emerson if she needs a Valium as I watch her get nervous. I know we will be kept to our schedule which means Emerson's dad should be meeting us shortly. A short while later, Valerie listens to something through her earpiece and announces, "Okay, ladies, let's get ourselves lined up like we did last night at the rehearsal."

As we line up to proceed, I'm floored by the overflow of guests who don't have seats in the church. Emerson had shared that Tina instructed them to invite a thousand people and they could expect maybe half to come to the mountains in Colorado. They were stunned when almost everyone who was invited responded that they were coming. It's one thing to know there are over a thousand guests, but to see it and then be the center of attention—even if only for a few moments—makes me extremely uncomfortable. Like Emerson, I worry about tripping and falling as I walk down the aisle in these sandals which are too tall.

It'll be a miracle if I don't have giant sweat stains on my dress by the time Emerson makes it to the front of the church. Wouldn't that be a pretty sight? I'm great with kids, less great with adults, and I'm terrible in crowds.

As we wait patiently, our flower girl, Amelie, sits on the bench, kicking her feet in the air as if she wishes she were on a swing. In the warm light of early fall, her hair glows chestnut, tumbling in curls down to the black dress she's wearing. Her brother, Jack, sits next to her, giving her a small poke in the stomach.

Valerie kneels next to the kids. "Hey, you guys. Ready to carry some flowers? And the ring pillow?"

The kids nod at Valerie. The little girl peers up at me, brown eyes wide. "I'm gonna ride my bike later. I've got a new helmet with lights on it, plus princesses and mermaids!" As she speaks, her cheeks dimple and eyes sparkle with pride. "My bike's pink. Do you have a bike?"

"I do. Maybe one day we can ride our bikes together. That sounds like a lot of fun. Now make sure you do what Miss Valerie says."

"I promise." She's ushered to the back of the line so she's standing in front of Emerson, who bends down to talk to the kids on their level. They hug her after a few moments, everyone clearly excited to get started.

My palms are getting wet, and I'm sure I'm going to hyperventilate. I can hear the buzz of the people in the church and spot people standing in the back. Valerie walks up with a bottle of water; I must look as nervous as I feel. I take tiny sips as we wait to walk down the aisle. I don't want to chew on my nails or lips, so I find myself gnawing on the inside of my cheek.

"Canon in D" begins, and my anxiety increases. Soon it'll be my turn to be front and center. I remind myself that they really are most interested in seeing Emerson walk down the aisle.

Out of the side of my eye, I spot Valerie signaling Siobhan to walk. I look back at Emerson; she's calm, cool, and collected. Me? I'm a wreck. I've been friends with Emerson ever since she became CeCe's roommate at Stanford when we were eighteen. She speaks at big events and is calm as a cucumber. Last night, they had us walk up and down the aisle a dozen times each to make sure we had the proper pace. I don't think I'll ever be able to walk down an aisle without thinking of Tina and her directions.

Sara's lined up, and she turns to me. "I think I more nervous than Emerson."

I mouth, "I know." My stomach is tight, and my nerves make me want to vomit.

I watch Sara as she's sent down the aisle. Greer's ready to go next. And before I realize it, she's gone and it's my turn. A thousand people look like ten thousand people to me. As I stand at the threshold of the church, I take a few breaths and say a small prayer that I don't stumble as I walk or that one of my breasts doesn't break free of my dress. I can hardly move, but then I feel a slight shove from behind. There are so many people in the church—standing room along the edges and the back of the church is all that is left. Every eye in the church is on me, my heart is racing, and I move. One foot in front of the other, I follow the beat like we were taught at the rehearsal.

I spot Cameron, and he beams at me. It should make me embarrassed, but it's almost as if telepathically he's talking to me, and I can ignore all the people and my fear of falling on my face. I immediately calm down and smile. Thankfully he doesn't break eye contact. I take a big breath when I arrive at the spot where I move to the left to stand in my appropriate place.

I didn't fall, and no exposed breast or nipples. Thank God!

I'm so nervous I don't notice CeCe as she walks up until she grasps my hand and gives me an assuring squeeze. The music changes to "A Midsummer Night's Dream: Wedding March." The entire church stands and watches Emerson make her grand entrance. The moment is perfect. Even with her veil, her smile lights up the room. Despite looking at the back of everyone's heads, I can hear the sniffles and see people dotting their faces with tissues. Dillon's standing tall and still a bit white, but when he sees Emerson, he visibly relaxes, his eyes sparkle, and his lips begin to curl. He appears so happy with a grin from ear to ear.

Emerson is stunning standing with her father next to her. I love weddings, and my eyes begin to water, but my makeup isn't waterproof, so I fight it. The crowd gives a collective "Ahh" and she proceeds, her eyes locked with Dillon. Both are smiling wide as she joins him. Her father moves the veil from her face and says something to Dillon, and he nods and shakes her father's hand.

As we all turn to the priest standing at the front, the mass begins. I'm not Catholic, but I went to a few services over the years. It's a beautiful ceremony. The cantor is one of Emerson's sister-in-law's, her voice like an angel as she sings throughout the mass.

My mind drifts through the service. I think about my current boyfriend, and I think about Cameron. I want to get married one day, and I hope to have at least two kids, but at the rate I'm going, I may have to adopt. Today is beautiful, and perfect for Emerson and Dillon, but this isn't for me. Too many people and, more importantly, too much pressure. *No, thank you.*

Emerson hands her bouquet of red roses to CeCe. I'm anxious and excited. I take a peek at Cameron, and his lips curl. Again, he calms me. The priest begins, "May I have the rings."

The ring bearer presents the pillow to the priest with the rings attached. He looks at Dillon and Emerson. "I believe there's a ring missing."

Dillon's is still on the pillow tied by a ribbon, but Emerson's 18-karat sapphire ring that is joined to the wedding band and was attached to the pillow is now missing.

This brings the ceremony to a complete halt.

Holy crap! What happened to the ring? Like everyone else, we're are all scrambling looking for it.

Emerson's mother can be heard over the murmurs asking, "How did that happen?"

"It appears to have come untied from the pillow," her dad replies.

Tina and her team are frantically searching around the back of the church. It's bedlam and Tina, who prides herself on her organization, appears as if she may cry. CeCe and I are staring at the ground, pacing back and forth trying to find where the ring could've rolled off and found a new home. Guests are in the aisle, and everyone is hunting frantically. It's a big ring so it shouldn't be hard to miss. Dillon and Emerson are standing at the altar holding hands, looking as if they don't know what to do.

After what is only moments but seems like minutes, Emerson's dad announces, "Here it is!" He holds it up for all to see, and there's a collective sigh in the church. Handing it to the priest, he explains, "It was hidden between the carpet runner and the edge of the pew, just out of sight."

"Jack, you did a great job. Next time, maybe a little less drama," Dillon says loud enough for everyone to hear

Jack looks like he's going to cry, and Emerson reaches down and gives him a hug. "Don't worry, big guy. Everything's okay. We found it."

The entire church laughs, and the rest of the ceremony goes without an issue. When Emerson and Dillon exchange their vows, CeCe removes a handkerchief from her bouquet stems and wipes her eyes, whispering, "I'm such a sucker for crying at weddings."

I reach for her hand and give it a squeeze.

When the recession begins, Dillon walks Emerson out, followed by CeCe and Mason. I watch them and think what a perfect couple they'd make. I've had the opportunity to get to know Mason on occasion; he's so self-assured and confident, which adds to his attractiveness.

When Cameron and I walk down the aisle, my stomach begins to turn, and my palms are sweating. He squeezes my arm tight and says, "You're doing great." As I gaze at the audience, I don't recognize many people as we slowly walk. Cameron must sense my nervousness and, just under his breath, he begins sharing with me who various people are who are sitting in the church. Many are clients of SHN. "To your right in the purple dress is Cindy Chou. She founded Fashion, the app. Sitting two rows up in that atrocious pinstripe suit is Brett Benedict. He's the founder of TubeIt. The beautiful blonde in the light blue dress is sitting next to Tom Sutterland, founder of PeopleMover."

I curl my fingers tightly around the bouquet as if I'm going to pop the heads of the roses off. If I didn't like this guy, I'd be funny and flirtatious, but since I do, my mouth is full of sawdust and my brain's malfunctioning as much as if I were drunk.

The bridal party is ushered to a private room while Tina grabs both Emerson's and Dillon's families for pictures. Meanwhile, her team pushes people along to the gondola and up the mountain to the top of Breckenridge for the reception.

chapter
TWO

CAMERON

AFTER ABOUT AN HOUR of additional photos, we're seated in several cars that caravan to the gondola, which we ride to the midpoint of Breckenridge Mountain and Ten-Mile Station. I'm disappointed that I didn't get to ride with Hadlee. When I saw her in her bridesmaid dress before leaving the hotel, I thought for sure she was going to catch my raging hard-on. She looked so hot in her dress. When I touched her back, I'm sure we both sensed the same electrical current.

Mason and I ride up the gondola, and we're directed by the wedding planner to a private room for the bridal party while we wait for the bride and groom to arrive. Everyone is talking together. I sit next to Hadlee, and I can feel the heat emanating from her body.

"We made it," I tell her.

She gives a brilliant white smile. "Thanks to you."

"I didn't have anything to do with it."

She moves a few inches closer and quietly says, "I have a total fear of large crowds like that. I don't think I would've been able to make it there and back to the altar without you." She shivers.

"Are you cold?"

"Do you want to know my special power?"

That seems like an odd question, but I'll bite. "Okay. Sure."

"The air conditioning vent will find me in any room and blow directly on me. So, if you're ever hot, come stand by me. And I'll also always find the leg of the table when I sit with a large group."

That is hilarious. Laughing, I stand and remove my coat, placing it over her shoulders. "Maybe this will help."

"You're very sweet. Thank you." She stares at her fingers. I notice they're long and delicate. I wonder what they'd look like wrapped around my dick.

Before I can get too caught up in my daydream, she asks, "What's your special power?"

"Well, I'm not sure I have the ability to direct air conditioning in a room or magically move the table around so only I'm inconvenienced. Let's think. I don't suppose finding a mistake in thousands of lines of code is a special power?"

With a singsong lilt to her voice, she says, "Nope. That's work-related. You're a master at your work, and everyone knows it. What's something that no one really knows about you that you do well?"

"Hmmm." I think about it a few moments and finally figure it out. "I'm able to spot a woman in distress from across the room and save her."

She stares at me, eyes wide. "That is so true. You saw how nervous I was at the wedding and to calm me, you caught my eye as I walked in. And then on the way out, you relaxed me by pointing out who some of the guests were. That was, simply put, perfect."

Her surprise and adulation have my cock on alert. I was really only kidding—my special power is actually how to destroy relationships with women—but I'll take it.

She snuggles in closer and says, "Thank you for that."

I put my arm around her and rub my hand along her arm to produce some friction heat. She smells wonderful, and I'm about to ask her if she'll hang with me during the reception when Tina announces, "Emerson and Dillon have arrived. Everyone ready to join the party?"

We nod, and she isn't happy with our response. "I want to hear that you're ready." Then this five-foot woman in four-inch heels yells at the top of her voice, "Are you ready to join the party?"

With as much enthusiasm as I can muster, I join the rest of the wedding party and scream, "Yes!"

Tina pairs us up to enter the grand ballroom the same way the girls entered the church, talking to each couple before they enter. When she gets to us, she says, "Okay, you two, the MC is going to play 'Happy' when you enter the room. Dillon and Emerson have provided a clever intro for him to say while you walk to the center. When you get to the dance floor, if you can dance a few moments and enjoy some time together, that would be ideal. You'll have a minute. Don't rush it, and show the guests you're having a great time."

Hadlee stares at me, and I know she's absolutely terrified. She's just told me large crowds scare her, and now they want her to do this?

I turn to her. "We're going to do great. We're going to hear them announce our names, and 'Happy' is an upbeat song, so you don't have to worry about me stepping on your toes with these giant clodhoppers."

She looks at my feet, takes a deep breath, and says, "Okay. We can do this."

Greer and her groomsman entered to AC/DC's "Back in Black." He's on his hands and knees in the middle of the dance floor, and she has a heel on his back and is pretending to whip him in a faux-BDSM ritual. The crowd is eating it up.

I hear Hadlee mutter, "We're going to look like idiots."

"No we're not. Follow my lead." "Happy" begins and the MC announces, "Please welcome Hadlee Ford. She's one of San Francisco's leading pediatricians during the day, and at night we can find her skipping along the waterfront. Cameron is a fellow founder of SHN, and when he isn't advising some of you on your technology, he's riding his Harley and dodging the law."

The crowd laughs, and I grab her hand. I took some dance lessons to impress a girl a long time ago, and while I'm not sure I remember, at least I'll be the one looking like a fool if this doesn't work. I spin Hadlee like a ballroom dancer, and she's like putty in my arms. It's like we'd practiced for hours. Of course, sixty seconds of spinning someone around a dance floor and a quick dip is easy to do without seeming too much like an idiot, thank God.

Only Hadlee and I understand that the terror was real, but it looked planned.

When we reach the rest of the bridal party, Hadlee has yet to release my hand. She leans in, pushing her soft breasts against my arm, and whispers, "You tricked me. You said you weren't a dancer. You were incredible."

"I took one dance class with Madame Trudeau with a girl years ago, and it all came back to me."

"You were certainly impressive."

Mason and CeCe just entered the room to "Uptown Funk," and they're jamming. Wow, there's definitely chemistry there. Everyone can tell they're having a blast.

I whisper in Hadlee's ear, "That's another couple who seems like they belong together. CeCe would be a really good match for him."

She squeezes my arm. "I agree."

We take our place at the head table, the room buzzing with excited chatter as some of the nieces and nephews run between the tables in a good-natured game of tag.

"At Last" by Etta James begins, and the MC grabs the microphone. "Ladies and gentlemen, may I introduce you to Mr. and Mrs. Dillon Healy." They arrive holding hands and smiling from ear to ear as applause spreads across the room. There's the scraping of chairs as folks rise for a standing ovation, and the happy couple make their way to the head table. They sit in front of a bouquet of deep red roses and Dillon leans in for a kiss, cheers and whoops rising from the crowd.

After a few moments, everyone sits and Mason rises from his chair, rapping his teaspoon on the side of his wineglass. He welcomes everyone and gives a wonderful toast to the couple. CeCe follows with her own toast, and then the waiters come out bearing trays laden with food. It really is a nice wedding, if you're into weddings.

Dinner is spectacular. I love good food, and I'm surprised when everyone in the room gets a plate with a filet mignon, a nice piece of salmon, a twice-baked potato and a heaping portion of sautéed broccoli.

As the dinner ends and the party begins, I watch Hadlee walk over to a gentleman who kisses her on her cheek. A pang of disappointment runs through me.

Turning to Mason, I ask, "Hey. I'm going to grab a drink. Need one?"

"Sure. I should get one for Annabel."

I stop in my tracks. *Mason brought a date?* My mind doesn't comprehend that. He's never mentioned seeing anyone before. Then it dawns on me. "Annabel? From legal?"

"Yeah, she's my date this weekend." He shrugs as if I'm the last one to know he's been banging the legal assistant.

I don't know if I'm simply upset that I seem to be the only person without a date this weekend, but I understand sexual harassment is serious business. "Dude. You're the rule enforcer. Why did you hook up with her?"

As if it's clear to everyone, he says, "She's cute."

"Yeah, but she works for you," I state the obvious.

"I know. She's hunting for a new job."

I'm still stunned by the news. This is a destination wedding. We live in San Francisco, and we're here in the mountains of Colorado. This was not a quick "Hey, you want to come with me to this wedding tomorrow?"

"Does Sara know?"

"Well, she knows now." He walks off and finds Annabel. She's pretty, but she's not for Mason. He needs someone who'll complement him and is as powerful and successful as he is.

This is a mess.

I believe it's gonna be a problem, but I'm not going to address the sexual harassment case that could be heading our way. We're here to celebrate Emerson's and Dillon's marriage, not deal with possible work issues.

I stand in line for drinks and remember standing at the front of the church and watching the bridesmaids march up the aisle. My heart stopped when I saw her. Hadlee was a pure vision—she has beautiful long auburn hair that I can imagine holding onto during sex. Her eyes are a perfect cerulean blue from the crayon box. She has the longest pair of legs, which in her dress seem to go on forever. And those round hips, heart-shaped ass with the perfect amount of jiggle, and mind-blowing tits that are obviously 100 percent real are enough to do me in right now. I've often wondered what her nipples look like and what it would be like to play with them. She takes my breath away.

She's everything I like physically in a woman, yet our social lives leave her off-limits. Every time I've ever seen Hadlee, I've reminded myself that she's friends with many of the people I work with. Getting involved with her could prove difficult should things go south, and with my screwed-up history, everything goes bad.

Our group of friends has mixed because of Dillon and Emerson. She joined our company almost three years ago, and with her came three stunning women and an introduction to the Arnault family. The first time I met Hadlee, I was surprised to learn she's one of the leading pediatricians in San Francisco and the great-granddaughter of one of the world's largest hotel chain founders. I'm pretty tech savvy and was able to do a little reconnaissance on the girls, and they each impressed me with their accomplishments. Hadlee specifically because she doesn't come across as a know-it-all doctor or even a trust-fund baby; she's warm and engaging and always quick to grin. She also allows CeCe to be the center of attention without competing with her.

Her intoxicating beauty and beaming personality are so alluring, I found myself unexpectedly staring at her a few times during the ceremony. Each time she caught me staring, she blushed a beautiful shade of pink.

I really need to get my mind off sex. It's been a few months since I've been with anyone, and I think about it nonstop when I look at her.

The wedding was nice. I'm not a religious guy, so the full Catholic mass was a bit challenging to follow. It's like aerobics—stand up, sit down, hold hands, kneel and repeat. Okay, maybe I'm overly generalizing. I gave up on religion when my mother was killed when I was a teenager. I don't have anything against it, I'm just not happy with God. Hadlee arrived last night with some guy, though I don't know who he's trying to fool. He was more interested in the male bartender than he was her. His loss. Hadlee was beautiful, and he hardly paid her any attention. *Why is she with that guy?*

Following dinner, the music starts, and Dillon has the world-famous band Monkey Business performing. I thought they seemed familiar when I saw them sitting in the audience. The head of the band asks Dillon and Emerson to come to the dance floor, and I'm expecting their song "Happily Ever After," so I'm surprised when they cover "Can't Help Falling in Love with You" by Elvis Presley instead. Even for a guy, I'm a bit moved by the romanticism of the day.

When it's time for the wedding party to dance, my palms are sweaty, and I'm sure Hadlee can hear how fast my heart is racing. All because of her. When she steps into me, she's so close I can smell her perfume, and I want so much to discover where she dabs it. She's soft in all the right places. I keep thinking about my third-grade teacher so I don't get a raging hard-on. But when the lead MC cracks a joke, and she seductively laughs in my ear, I know she must realize it isn't something in my pocket.

When the song ends, I don't want to let her go. She glances up at me through her eyelashes and says, "I guess I should join my date."

"Oh yeah. Thanks for the dance." *Why did I say that? Good grief.* I should've manned up and told her to get rid of the gay guy, that I'd show her a good time. But I don't. Instead I find a drink and wander out to the balcony. The views from here of the Colorado Rockies and the valley below are outstanding. The air is crisp with the smell of winter approaching. I bet this place is stunning covered in snow.

God, I hate this.

chapter
THREE

HADLEE

MY BOYFRIEND DEREK LIKES THE BARTENDER. We met each other on matchme.com a few months ago, and he was very open about having recently left a long-term relationship with another man but told me he wanted to get married and have children. I love children—I am pediatrician, for God's sake. We get along really well, but his hitting on the bartender all night has me convinced that he's really only looking for a beard for a wife, and I want something more. We've never even had sex, and I was hoping this would be the weekend.

When he brings me my third drink, I ask, "So, what's the bartender's name?"

"John. Do you mind if I hang out with him tonight?" His eyes light up for this guy and not for me. It's time I face reality. If I'm going to get involved with Derek, it means I'm giving up on love, and I'm not ready to do that.

"Derek, why did you come with me to this wedding?"

"Because you asked me to." He gazes at me and carefully says, "You know I have feelings for you, Hadlee."

Trying hard to be diplomatic, I tell him, "I think when we

return to San Francisco, we're going to have to go our separate ways."

"What! Why?"

"Derek, I understand your family wants you to be married and have a lot of kids, but you can do that with a man. You'll be happier being the real you."

"Hadlee, you know my parents would never accept a gay lifestyle. Please, I'm begging you. Please don't break up with me."

"I'll get another room tonight." I stand up, trying to scrape together what little dignity I have right now. Here I am at this remarkable wedding where two of my closest friends have just married, where everyone around me is having a wonderful time, and my date is asking for permission to sleep with a man.

How did I go so wrong in this life?

As I gather the last of my things, he stops me. "Wait. Is there anything I can do to change your mind?"

I shake my head. "No, I don't think so."

I walk away at that point and head to the front desk. "I seem to need a second room. I'm with the Winthrop/Healy wedding."

The clerk clicks a few buttons on the computer and then scrutinizes me. "I'm so sorry. We're sold out."

My stomach drops. "Oh crap. Really? What am I going to do?" I'm close to crying. I can't stay with Derek. CeCe left early. Emerson is newly married. Sara is with Trey, her fiancé, and Greer has disappeared, too.

"Let me call around and see who might have a room. The wedding has several places reserved throughout the area."

"That would be great. I appreciate your help. I can wait over here."

What am I going to do if I can't get a room?

I watch her make call after call. Finally, she says, "Ms. Ford? I'm so sorry, but I've called all the reputable places here in Breckenridge, Frisco, Keystone, and the town of Dillon, and I'm not finding any available rooms for tonight."

Crap!

I wander back into the party, which is still going strong. I ask the wedding planner if she has any suggestions and she tells me she doesn't.

Cameron overhears and asks, "You gave that guy your room?"

I'm mad at myself, and I want to scream, "Yes, I'm that stupid." Instead, I try to muster as much dignity as I can. "Thanks, Cameron. Rub it in." Glancing around for CeCe or one of my friends so I can crash on their couch, I don't spot anyone. I walk over to the bar and order another drink, though what I really want to do is cry in the corner.

Cameron follows me to the bar. "Please don't get upset."

"Cameron, I appreciate that you mean well, but I really can't take anyone giving me a hard time tonight."

"I'm sorry. I'm not trying to give you a hard time." His attention lingers on my pearl necklace before trailing to my cleavage. I exhale slowly when his eyes move up to my throat and jawline, then to my hair before returning to meet mine. "Please stay with me. You can have the bed, and I can sleep on the floor."

"I'm not sure that's a good idea," I whisper.

Reaching for my hand, he growls, "I insist."

I don't really have much choice. I nod, and he leads me to the elevators. When we arrive at his room, he politely opens the door, and I pass through. It's nothing more than a plain room with a king-size bed. No couch.

I can sleep on the floor. At least it isn't the couch in the lobby for everyone to see my stunning failure.

Excusing himself, he goes into the bathroom. I didn't think this through, and I don't have much more than my bridesmaid dress. I sit on the bed and wait. He exits the bathroom in just a pair of boxers, and it's even better than I imagined. With broad shoulders, a deep tan, his torso covered in tattoos, smoldering eyes, a strong jaw, and a head of straight-out-of-bed, vogue-cool, catwalk hair that flops onto his forehead, he looks like one of those totally hot and brooding Abercrombie and Fitch models, only more savage and fierce.

"What, no baseball hat?"

He lets out a deep belly laugh and runs his hands through his hair. "I guess I do wear them a lot. I have a lot of hair."

I'm not usually this bold. CeCe is the bold one, not me. It may be the alcohol talking, but I don't think it is. I've had a serious crush on Cameron since we met, and I want him.

I need him.

I stare at his chest, my eyes lingering on the dragon that takes up his torso and most of his arms. He's positively beautiful. We've never explored anything. In fact, we've never exchanged anything more than pleasantries. My eyes wander across his chest and up his arms. He watches me carefully, and his cock stirs in his boxers. I didn't even realize I'd licked my lips until he says, "If you don't stop, I won't be able to sleep on the floor."

"I'm not sure I want you to sleep on the floor," I purr. I've never had a one-night stand, but if that's all we have, then that's what I want. He's making my insides clench with want. I need him more than I need air right now.

He gazes at me with desire-filled eyes. “I'm serious, Hadlee. You're a beautiful woman, and I won't be able to control myself.”

I rise from the bed, and he watches me carefully as I approach. Stepping into his space, I run my fingers over the dragon. I hear his breath catch. “You promise not to be able to control yourself?”

With no warning, his mouth crashes over mine. His soft, sensual lips feel so damn good as his seductive kiss teases me, and then he taunts me with the tip of his tongue, willing my mouth to open for him.

“Mmm,” he moans as he tilts his head so he can work those lips on mine from a better angle.

I'm caving quickly, and for the love of all that's holy, I want a taste of him.

chapter
FOUR

CAMERON

HER GOWN FALLS TO THE FLOOR in a swoosh and pools at her feet. I stand up and take a step back, reveling in the exquisite beauty before me. Her eyes never leave mine. She's curvy with large exquisite breasts, fine pink nipples begging to be toyed with, her small waist held tight with a corset, and a sexy, tiny pair of panties. She shivers from the chill of the room, or maybe with anticipation of the erection that's pushing hard against my boxer shorts.

I've wanted to feel her from the inside since I met her years ago, but she's always been off-limits. I'm the type of guy who doesn't really do relationships; I like to bang them hard and move on to the next girl. We have the same circle of friends, and this could become difficult. But as I look at her, I can't say no. I don't *want* to say no.

I want her.

I step forward and lean down. Our lips touch and begin their tango, her tongue dancing with mine unabashedly, and my heart leaps in my chest. She nips at my bottom lip and then slides her tongue over the injury, soothing me. I can't fucking breathe; her show of desire has me on fire. I pull her body in closer by the small of her back, angling my head so our tongues can explore each other with fervor. Her nipples harden against my chest, and a small whimper escapes her lips. The more we kiss, the more I need her like my next breath.

She really knows how to work her tongue. I shouldn't have kissed her, because my hormones are now kicking into overdrive. As my body instinctively takes over, my mouth waters at the thought of tasting her. I gently trail light, sensual, open-mouthed kisses along her ear and the length of her neck. She tastes like heaven, and my breathing picks up. This woman does something unexplainable to me, stirring emotions deep within. Emotions I haven't let surface in a long time.

I cup her abundant breast and suck the erect nipple into my mouth, sucking aggressively until she groans, her fist in my hair, pushing me in to her.

"You have the most beautiful tits."

"Play with them," she demands.

Her fingers move beneath her panties to her core, and I can hear how wet she's becoming as she moans with each movement. Removing her wet fingers from her pussy, I place them in my mouth, sucking at her juices. "Mmm... you taste so good."

Her breathing labors as my fingers replace hers. She reaches for my cock with her free hand and strokes me, driving me crazy.

Her panties dampen as I stroke the outside, and her nipples harden. I slip her panties off and tuck them out of sight while my fingertips dip inside, running along her skin, and her breathing becomes ragged. Her touch sends me spiraling as we both pant heavily with uncontrolled want. She's turning me on as she responds to me unashamedly, arching her tits into my hands. Running her fingers through my short hair, she pulls me deeper into the kiss.

"You have me on fire," she breathes over my lips. My thumb stroking her pebbled nipple, and she lets out a moan. Damn, the woman can kiss.

My hand's working at her core through her panties, I stop and ask, "Are you sure?"

"I've never been so sure of anything in my life."

Standing back, I take in her beautiful pussy. I can't wait to get in and taste it. But she has other ideas.

Taking my hard dick in her hands, she pushes me back onto the bed and shimmies between my legs. She slides her lips over the tip, moistening my cock as she takes as much of me as she can into her mouth. She sucks me, moving at a slow, steady pace guaranteed to drive me crazy. Her hand grips the base, sliding up and down below her mouth. She uses her free hand to cup my balls, feeling them drawn high and tight toward my body with arousal. In a husky whisper, I beg, "Squeeze them harder." She immediately does, and I'm in heaven.

I'm big in her mouth. Hadlee can't take all of me without gagging, so she plays to her strengths and teases the sensitive spot below the head of my cock. Finally, I reach to pull her up. "If you don't stop, I'll come before I get to fuck you. And I really, really want to fuck you."

I flip her around again so she's on her knees on the bed, then push her down by the back of her neck so she's bent over, ass up, ready for me. I can't help but take in her round hips and ass as I work my fingers in and out of her juicy pussy.

There's nothing romantic here—it's just pure, hot, and feral. She wants me as much as I want her. In two strides, I'm in the bathroom and have a condom from my shaving kit. I sheathe my cock quickly she seductively pulling at her nipples and playing with her slick pussy.

Adjusting her where I want her, her porcelain white ass positioned at just the right height, I thrust my throbbing cock inside her and she cries out in pleasure. Holding her hips, I continue my slow, powerful pumping into her needy pussy. She softly grunts each time I thrust deep into her, making me wish I could see the pleasure on her face in the reflection in the picture behind the bed. She matches my rhythm as she pushes her hips back to bring more of me into her.

"I don't want to come yet," I grunt between my thrusts. I want to enjoy this longer. Pulling out, I roll her over and open her pussy wide. I can't help but be further amazed at her beautiful pink, slick pussy.

I greedily lean in and lick her wetness, then push my tongue through her opening and sink into her core. I flick it in and out of her with long, languid strokes, tasting her. Her legs begin to quake uncontrollably as she grips the bedsheet tight. "I've only just begun," I breathe over her pussy. I gaze up at her, her eyes hooded, and slowly insert two fingers inside her. "You're so wet," I say in awe, my fingers working in and out of her core. Feeling her body building toward something sweet, I spread and turn my fingers around deep inside her, stretching her, and her mouth drops open as she moans. "Does that feel good, sweetheart?"

"Oh, Cameron," she pants. "Yes... that... feels... sooo... good."

Her orgasm is so strong it virtually squirts into my mouth. She tastes so sweet and musky. I lick up the nectar, not wanting to miss a drop. "Holy shit, that was fucking incredible."

"It's your turn," she tells me as she reaches between our bodies and takes me in her hand. God, her hand, so delicate but so assured on my dick. I slip my finger back inside her pussy, and she pumps me at the same tempo as I do her, showing me she can take it if I can. Not sure my body can take it, I fall to the bed beside her, fingers and hands still in place. Facing each other, we work one another into a frenzy, our breath mingling in the small space between us. Together we speed up, until we're both crying out, feeling the release together.

Glancing at the clock, I see it's after three o'clock. I'm exhausted yet exhilarated. She's astonishing. "Give me a few. I want to do that again."

She nods her agreement, and I grin.

That was so much better than I ever expected.

We drift to sleep wrapped in each other's arms.

chapter
FIVE

HADLEE

I HEAR MY CELL PHONE PING, indicating a text, but it doesn't register. When it pings a second time, I glance over at the clock—it's almost 9:00 a.m. My head's killing me and beating to an unknown dance beat. The slight crack in the window curtains is bright. Too bright.

Oh God, I have quite the hangover. Not so bad that I don't remember anything from last night though. In fact, I remember every glorious—and embarrassing—minute of it.

Rolling over, I notice Cameron with the sheets wrapped around his magnificent waist. He's delicious enough to eat. I chuckle, remembering having already done that in the last six hours.

My cell phone pings again. *Who's so desperate to get a hold of me?*

CeCe: WHERE ARE YOU?

CeCe: I went to your room this morning, and Derek said you broke up. WTF? Where are you?

I sit up, my head hurting even more than when I was horizontal. I text her back.

Me: Please don't worry. I'm fine. My head's killing me. Give me a few minutes, and I'll meet you at your room and give you the 411.

CeCe: If you aren't here in ten minutes, I'm calling 911.

Me: I'm coming as fast as my headache will allow.

I slowly slip out of bed. I wouldn't have minded another round or three this morning, but I made breakfast plans with the girls knowing Derek and I wouldn't lounge around in bed. Cameron doesn't wake or even move a hair on his very fine body.

I grab one of his T-shirts and a pair of his workout shorts, but I can't find my panties. What did he do with them when he peeled them off me. I've searched under the bed and can't find them anywhere. I'm running out of time, so I decide to let it go and ask about them later. Piling my hair on my head, I drape my dress over my arm and make the walk of shame up to CeCe's room. At least I shouldn't run into anyone.

Arriving at CeCe's room, I bring my hand up to knock but she swings the door open and pulls me into the room. Greer and Sara are sitting on the bed.

"Are you okay?" they ask in unison.

I blush from head to foot. "Yes, I'm fine. I'm sorry I didn't call. Derek spent the night flirting with the bartender, and I felt like a fool."

"You have nothing to feel foolish about," Sara interjects, rubbing my back.

"I knew he had broken up with another man before we met, but he seemed so sincere that he wanted a straight relationship. I guess he only wanted a false one to make his parents happy."

“Honey, you understand better than any of us, that lifestyle isn’t a choice, it’s how he was born.”

“Thank you. I think it’s an occupational hazard, and I was desperate to find someone who said all the right things about having a family and having babies.”

They all get up and embrace me in a group hug.

“So where did you sleep last night? And where did those clothes come from?” CeCe asks.

“I got a little drunk, and a friend took me to their room since I couldn’t find one in the hotel, or even in the neighboring towns.” My head’s still pounding. I need a shower, and it’s then I realize I don’t have my suitcase. “Oh shit! My suitcase is in my old room.”

“Why didn’t you call me?”

“You left before I broke up with Derek. As far as I could tell, you left with some hot guy.”

“It was the exact opposite. I saw everyone coupling up and decided after Emerson and Dillon left the party that the Jacuzzi tub in my room was calling my name.”

I give her a hug of encouragement. “I’m sorry, sweetie. If you guys can give me fifteen minutes, I can take a shower, get all the hair spray out of this mess on my head, and then I’ll be ready for breakfast.

“I’ll go get your suitcase,” Greer offers.

Undressing in the bathroom, I look at my body. I have a bit of whisker burn on my breasts, but beyond that, I don’t look any different. I feel different though: excited, exhilarated, and my pussy is on fire—but in a good way. I don’t think anyone has ever made me feel the way Cameron does. I now get why a woman can go *Fatal Attraction* on a guy. Holy cow!

I shower and dress in casual clothes, and the four of us head to the dining room for breakfast. After we make small talk and order, we get to the nitty-gritty of talking about all the guests at the wedding.

Turning to Sara, I ask, "Doesn't Annabel work for you?"

Sounding disgusted, she says, "Yes. I wasn't aware she was dating the managing partner. That's going to create some challenges when we get back to San Francisco. She's had a crush on him for a while, but I didn't think he would be stupid enough to actually date her." She turns a shade of crimson. "I probably shouldn't have said that out loud."

"You're with friends. You're safe to share among us." CeCe reaches for Sara's hand and gives it a reassuring squeeze. "What a mess. Mason doesn't seem like the kind of guy who thinks with his dick, either."

"He's usually so much smarter than that," Sara agrees.

"She must give spectacular blowjobs," I say.

Everyone snickers.

"She's been pretty persistent," Sara states, "but I'm still at a loss."

Greer turns to me and says, "When I saw Cameron all dressed up, and without the baseball hat, I finally understood why you're so head over heels for him. He does clean up nice."

If she only knew. I'm going to feel all the fun we had last night for a few days.

My core clenches and my nipples pebble at the thought of what he did to me. My panties are wet just thinking about what I'm sure are magic fingers, and that tongue. Holy shit, I know what amazing sex is like now. I think I pulled a muscle.

Cameron's occupied my thoughts on a regular basis since I met him. I don't regret having slept with him. Quite the opposite, actually. I want to make my excuses and go back to him. There are so many things I'd like to explore. I feel so renewed and refreshed following all my orgasms. I want more of him. I want to feel like this again, and often.

"I told you. He's a good-looking guy once you get past the T-shirts, scruffy face, and faded jeans," Sara jokes.

I can't keep thinking of him. If I do, I'll go back to his room. Needing to change the subject, I ask CeCe, "When do Emerson and Dillon leave for their honeymoon in Greece?"

"They fly out this afternoon. They drove to Denver to stay in the Brown Palace Hotel last night."

With dreamy eyes, Greer says, "It was such a beautiful wedding."

We spend the rest of the morning talking about the ceremony and making notes for our future weddings. As we're discussing the missing ring, my cell phone pings.

Cameron: I was disappointed that you weren't here when I woke up this morning.

The girls don't seem to notice as I bite my lip, thinking of him in bed, naked with a raging hard-on, and how I wouldn't mind writhing beneath him and scratching at the dragon on his chest.

Me: Sorry. The girls were searching for me, and I didn't want to disturb you.

Cameron: Because you knew if you did, we'd still be in bed now.

My body reacts to the thought of his mouth playing with my

nipples, his fingers buried deep inside me. Maybe I can find an excuse to go back and spend the day with him?

Me: The thought did occur to me. What are your plans today?

Cameron: I'm checking out shortly and heading on the first of two spectacular motorcycle rides I've been told about. What about you?

That's disappointing on so many levels. If he had asked me to come back and play, I probably would've made excuses. I don't usually have one-night stands, but he was incredible, and I need to keep this light so he doesn't worry that he'll have a crazy psycho on his hands.

Me: Shopping at the outlet malls, and I need to get some rest. There was a hot, painted man who kept me up all night.

Cameron: Painted? I like that.

I need to keep this light. Show him I can be discrete. Me: Enjoy your ride.

Cameron: I'd rather ride you. See you later.

How can he say that and not expect me to come running?

Me: (Fanning myself to keep cool.) Me too. Bye.

I'M A LITTLE DISAPPOINTED that he didn't invite me with him or make plans to go out—or stay in—when we return to San Francisco. Sure, I could've asked him about getting together when we get home, but maybe I've read too many books about guys. They like the thrill of the chase, and I wanted him to chase me. Still, I'm hopeful we can do that a few more dozen times. He was a-maz-ing!

Returning my attention to our brunch, I realize Trey's joined us, along with Mason and Annabel.

"This has been a fantastic trip." Annabel grins and giggles, staring at Mason, who blushes and can't make eye contact with any of us.

Okay, this is awkward and bordering on gross. I look across the table and see the look on CeCe's face. Her smile is forced. I want to shake Mason and ask, "What the hell are you thinking?" Then I look at Sara, and I can tell she's struggling. I don't think any of us will understand what he sees in Annabel.

Sara is able to pull it together quickly and asks them, "What are your plans today?"

"We're driving into Aspen for a sunset hot air balloon ride," Annabel announces proudly.

"That sounds wonderfully romantic," I tell them.

She nods vigorously. "That's what I think, too."

Sara has a pained expression, and I can only imagine it's because Annabel works for her as her legal assistant.

Changing the subject, I ask, "What are your plans, Sara?"

She quietly responds, "We're going horseback riding at a ranch not far from here."

"Oh, that sounds fun."

Trey gazes at her. "Sara's never seen a horse up close in person."

I pat her on the leg to soothe her obvious anxiousness. "You grew up in San Francisco, like me. I don't think I saw a horse up close until I went to sleep-away camp when I was fifteen."

Sara has a look of relief, and CeCe mouths, "Thank you."

Trey turns to Sara and grasps her hand tightly. "See, sweetheart? Nothing to be embarrassed about."

CeCe sighs. "I wish I could join you both, but Hadlee, Greer, and I are planning to do a bit of shopping and hitting the spa here at the hotel. We have massages at three."

"I also booked a facial and mani-pedi. Do either of you care for one?" Greer asks.

CeCe looks down at her hands, inspecting her nails. "I just did those before I left."

"Me, too," I add.

I'm surprised when Cameron wanders in and then comes over to the table. I thought he was in bed texting me, but he's obviously freshly showered and ready to tackle the day. Good Lord, the man's a work of art, and his ass—holy hell. The way his jeans tightly hug his backside... oh my.

The group welcomes him, and he pulls a chair up next to me. Everyone is busy in various conversations when he leans in and whispers in my ear, "I found your panties."

My heart races. "I'd offer to come take them off your hands, but I believe you've already checked out, and I still don't have a hotel room."

His eyes are smoldering. "I have, but I packed them away and will get them to you at home. They seem like they're probably part of a very sexy set."

His fingers are making small circles on my thigh, and I can't take much more. He's attacking all my senses, and I'm completely powerless to him. "Maybe we can meet up when you get back to San Francisco?"

He beams at me and squeezes my leg beneath the table. My stomach lurches, and I'm sure I have a wet spot between my legs.

Standing, he announces, "All right, gang. This has been a fun weekend, but I have two bike rides ahead of me, and then I ride home."

"You're riding home?" Greer asks, eyes wide.

"Why not? Are you worried I'm not coming back?"

"Well... of course not. I just...."

He leans over and kisses her on the cheek. "I'm just giving you a hard time, Greer. I haven't taken any time away from work since we started, and I finally have the team in place to do so. I thought everyone knew I was taking the long way back to San Francisco."

A little green monster rears its head with their small amount of intimacy. I realize they work together and I've been told Cameron's a technical genius and Greer's able to dissect the technical into uncomplicated words so someone like me can understand. Greer's my friend, and she's known for a long time that I've been crazy about Cameron, but I'm still a little jealous of how close they are. All of them are close, actually; I'm the odd man out.

SHN is one of the leading venture capital firms in the Bay Area, and as I look around the table, everyone seems to work for them in one capacity or another except for me. I've been friends with CeCe since we were in preschool. She, her brother, and father are advisors to the partners, and they get together at their parents' house most Sunday nights. Dillon, Mason, and Cameron are founding partners, having started the company. Sara, Emerson, and Greer are partners, and recently they extended an offer to another who I haven't met yet. Sometimes I feel a little left out when they talk business, but other times I'm glad not to have the troubles that seem to plague them.

Cameron stands to leave, positioning himself behind me while he says goodbye to everyone and gives me a quick squeeze.

CeCe doesn't miss anything. Muttering under her breath, she says, "I think you need to tell me more about last night."

I smile and nod. I'm sure I can give her the PG-rated version.

The group slowly breaks off to their respective activities, leaving Greer, CeCe, and me. CeCe looks at me carefully. "Okay, missy. Spill. Did you spend last night with Cameron?"

Greer stamps her feet and screeches a happy sound.

I don't want to kiss and tell. I want to savor this for a while and enjoy what we did. "He was kind enough to give me a place to stay last night. It isn't a big deal."

"That's bullshit. We've been friends since we were five years old. Tell us more."

"I can only share that he has the most beautiful dragon tattoo on his chest."

"His total chest is a dragon?" Greer asks.

"It is, and it swirls around his back. His arms are also covered. One has beautiful flames from the dragon's mouth, and the other has some wonderful designs. It's really pretty stunning."

"But you can't tell he has anything on his chest only his arms are covered to just above his wrists."

"He can wear a dress shirt and roll the sleeves up to his mid arm, and no one would know." Remembering last night and the dull ache between my legs right now, I continue, "He hides them rather well."

CeCe leans in just loud enough for the table to hear and asks, "But how are his other skills?"

"What time can we arrive at the spa?" I ask, ready to move on.

"Nice try. I'm very happy for you, and if he hurts you in any way, I'll break him," CeCe assures me.

She's known me virtually all my life and is wonderfully protective. I know she would make Cameron's life miserable if he hurt me, but for right now, we've only had one night of amazing sex and no concrete plans for anything else. I want to enjoy this without hours of girlfriends overanalyzing our every move. "Ladies, we have no commitment. Not even plans to go out again when we return home."

"We're all friends," Greer chimes in. "You'll be able to spend more time together. And maybe you'll stay in rather than go out."

I cut my eyes to her. "Rarely do I hang out with all of you. You all work together. I'm a pediatrician whose office is across town."

"We can work on that." She squeezes my arm and winks at me.

I'm sure I'll soon regret that they know.

chapter SIX

CAMERON

I DRESS IN MY LEATHERS—chaps I wear over my jeans—big steel-toed boots, a jacket, and gloves. It isn't that I fear an accident; I'm an excellent driver and pay close attention while I'm on the road. Unfortunately, many drivers don't pay attention outside the bubble of their cars and can miss motorcycles. Road rash hurts like a son of a bitch, and I prefer the leather take a beating over my skin.

Placing my skull helmet on, I start up my bike. It roars to life in a way only a Harley can.

Seated on the Harley Fat Boy, I listen to the purr of the engine. It stirs something inside me. I know some find the Harley loud and distracting, but to me, the sound is relaxing white noise; I can block out the world and think.

As I leave the resort, I head for the mountain roads. Once there, I disregard the speed limit and open the throttle wide. Sometimes my knee skims the ground as I take the bends in the road. I have a hard job, and this is my therapy. I love it.

Riding is a combination of exhilaration, fear, relaxation, and pleasure that changes you forever. There's something to be said about the freedom of nothing between you and the air at eighty-five miles per hour. It's the closest thing to flying I'll experience while still being on the ground. It's physical and emotional pleasure, with a layer of anxiety and adrenaline. I smell everything—diesel, rain, hamburgers, whatever's in the air where I'm riding. I feel every nuance of weather as I ride and elevations change: temperature, moisture, everything. My favorite is the white noise. The wind, your bike, it all combines into this generic sound. This is where I find my peace. Where I think the very best.

When I woke this morning, my cock was hard as a lead pipe and throbbing. I would've loved to have Hadlee to take care of it. Unfortunately, she smartly went to her friends. I've always found her hot as hell, and the sex was intense, but she may not enjoy the sex I've come to like. I want to feel something that doesn't come from the traditional. It's pretty simple—I like kinkier sex than most women seem to want.

I do have her panties. It may've been a mistake to have fucked her, but I'm still a man, and she was certainly all woman. She was vulnerable and looking at me and licking her lips. I warned her and gave her a choice. I do need to be honest with myself though. It would most definitely be fun to do a repeat, but she's within my social circle, so that may be a mistake.

Thankfully, I don't have to make the decision now.

The look on her face when I walked into the dining room was priceless. It reminded me of the one when she reaches her pinnacle. That glorious moment. The girls didn't mention her staying in my room, so I'm confident that she hasn't said anything to them. I like sharing a secret with her.

Maneuvering myself down the mountain into Denver, I follow the directions to meet the first motorcycle club. Before I left

San Francisco, I reached out to two different clubs and set myself up for two rides. The first is with the Colorado club out of Denver. They have a full-day ride this morning that'll take us into Rocky Mountain National Park. I grew up in Northern California and haven't had a chance to explore the world. This is my opportunity to enjoy what I've only seen in magazines or movies. The plan is to spend the night in Winter Park and in the morning, I'll head north on the back roads to Wyoming. I'll then meet a club outside of Jackson Hole. Our plan is to ride through Yosemite for three days, which is the trip I'm most excited about. I'm hoping to see some wildlife and enjoy the park. It should be a good time.

From there I'll head home. In all, I'll be gone two weeks. I've needed a vacation for a while, and my plan was to sleep with as many women as I could find on this trip, but after my night with Hadlee, I'm not sure I'm interested.

How did that happen?

chapter
SEVEN

HADLEE

It's time to return to work, and I'm ready. The long weekend in Colorado was fun, my time with Cameron unexpected, but it's time to get back to reality.

I love being a pediatrician. Staring at my patient schedule for today, I have twenty-five appointments, and usually a few more will get squeezed in throughout the day for sick visits. My Spanish will be getting a workout. Almost all of my patients speak Spanish as a first language.

Despite the bright and colorful Dr. Seuss paintings on the walls throughout our practice, my patients are mobile and spry, bored, yet grinning each time I enter an exam room. Parents tend to be stressed and exhausted.

Before I entered the room, Maria, my medical assistant, warned me that my patient is nervous. I watch her play with the otoscope. Her mother hisses her name as a reprimand, "Cynthia."

Making her feel comfortable is my job, and I know just what to say. I reach my hand out to my patient, I say, *"Hola Doctora, soy Doctora Hadlee. Debes ser el nuevo doctor. ¿Cómo te llamas?"*

"Cynthia," she tells me shyly.

Winking at the mother, I ask her in Spanish, "Oh, then are you the patient today?" She appears puzzled by my ruse, and I nod to encourage her. She tells me "*Sí.*"

Pointing to Cynthia, I ask, "Can you tell me what's wrong with our patient?"

Cynthia isn't sure what to do, and her mother says, "Tell her what feels bad."

Cynthia then lightens up and shares with me a litany of her ailments, mostly that she has a sore throat. I ask questions to verify, and it looks like she has strep. I do a quick swab, but even the smell tells me it's strep.

I explain, "I have a good Z-pack sample that should have you back to school in no time." Our practice is very lucky, and we work hard to make sure our patients get the care they need. Most of our patients are on Medicaid, which can often mean the visit is very low cost, but the medication may come at a price. Our pharmaceutical reps are very good to us and give us samples regularly, which we give to those who need it.

They thank me and they're off. The rest of my day is similar, twenty-four more patients with ear infections, sore throats, coughs, and one of my favorite family's daughter who's tired and can't shake the exhaustion. It's a normal day.

When I get home, I check my messages, but there's nothing from Cameron. I can't help but be disappointed. I know he isn't home for two weeks, but a girl can hope she isn't far from his mind. It'd been a long time since I'd had good sex, and sex with Cameron was better than good. I want more from him.

Getting undressed, I catch a glimpse of my body in the mirror and think of the things he did to me. I begin to play with my nipples; remembering his touch, they're hard and wanting more. I gently twist and pull them, and they send an electrical current directly to my core until I'm completely aroused.

I lie on my bed and my fingers find my clit, slowly circling it while my other hand continues with my nipples. I imagine it's Cameron doing this to me as I remember our time together, the smell of his cologne and the slight scratch of his two-day-old stubble. I move my thumb and forefinger against the nubs of my nipples a little harder and a little faster.

Closing my eyes, I groan a low guttural sound. God, I need this badly. With my right hand still massaging my breast, the left continues to play with my clit. Chills sweep through my body at the mere touch. My middle finger curls inside my sex, feeling the wetness inside me. My index finger joins the first, and I begin to slowly slide my fingers inside my slick hole. Squeezing my breast sends shivers to my pussy, and I moan as I work my fingers in and out. The sounds are music to my ears.

I spread my knees farther apart in concentrated pleasure as I pick up speed. A stray finger finds my clit and starts to rub in vicious circles as I imagine he's there with me. I groan a deep animal noise as my orgasm hits, and I come powerfully, my pussy climaxing over my fingers. I relish the waves of sensual bliss overtaking me, traveling throughout my body.

I'm out of breath as I lie here, completely spent.

I need him.

chapter EIGHT

CAMERON

"DUDE! YOU'RE BACK," says one of my team members as I exit the elevator to the lobby of our offices. I'm certain he was waiting for me.

I'm glad to be back, but I needed the break, and I'm recharged. Mason, Dillon, and I are the three founding partners at SHN. This was the first time in almost a decade that I took any significant time away from the office. We began funding start-ups together as a hobby after the three of us had success at the ones where we worked. Over a round of drinks at a pub one afternoon, we decided it was time to pool our resources and share some of our luck, giving seed or angel funding to projects we liked as a side gig to our regular jobs. When four of our investments were bought for millions of dollars each, we quickly became addicted to the gamble and the high of identifying a winner when investing in an exciting idea, and we started our own fund. Since inception, we've invested in three hundred start-ups, and we're still going strong.

"It was a great week. Colorado and Yosemite were beautiful. How did things go while I was out?"

"Everything went according to plan."

Annabel sashays up. "Hey, Cameron, Mason's looking for you."

Before I can help myself, I ask, "Are you now going to mother us?"

She giggles. "No, silly. I just left his office, and he mentioned he was excited to see you when you returned today." She licks her lips, and it grosses me out a bit to think what she was doing with my friend.

"Oh. Thanks."

I walk into our break room, and there's a big breakfast spread on the center island—my favorite, pancakes and blueberry syrup. Piling a healthy helping on a plate and drowning them in butter and syrup, I walk into Mason's office.

"Hey, man. Your woman told me you were searching for me."

"Great. How was your trip?"

"Good. Look, I think we need to have a conversation about your relationship with Annabel with the team and Charles on Sunday."

"Why?"

"Man, the fact that you have to ask is reason enough. Do you plan on making her a partner next?"

"I understand it's a bit unordinary, and honestly I don't know what we are right now." Shrugging, he says, "She pursued me and is into me, and I think she's cute."

"I think we need to discuss this as a team. Sara must be coming unglued right now."

"Relax. Annabel promised to keep it professional."

"Don't you understand that they always say that until they're unhappy—either in their job or with their relationship."

"I already spoke to Sara, and she's okay with it."

Given the last conversation in Colorado, I don't think that's the case, but I'm not going to argue with him. We can discuss it as a team later. I don't want to fight. "Great. What else do you need from me?"

"I wanted to make sure you reached out to our investigator on the mole issue. He seemed to have some leads for us from the recent acquisitions."

"I'll do that."

With that, I leave, thinking Mason is usually so much smarter. I wish I knew what the hell he was thinking. He's not a guy usually guided by his dick, but I can't think of any other reason why he's doing this.

I open my e-mail to find over six hundred messages. Thankfully, my team and admin watched them while I was out, so there are only about two dozen that need my immediate attention.

After figuring out my plan, I finally reach out to Jim, our private investigator.

A few years ago, we started seeing some of our business mysteriously going to a competitor. We figured we had an internal mole and hired a private investigator who specialized in corporate espionage. After a meeting with a tech company that went well, the next day our entire proposal and financial models were released to the press, and things imploded a little over a year ago. It could've been disastrous, but thankfully we had Greer on our team, and she created a strong public relations counter blitz. The information still hurt us financially, but it didn't force us to close. We've changed some things up since then, and we work extensively with our private investigator and his security team.

Jim answers after the first ring. "Jim Peterson."

"Hey, this is Cameron Newhouse. I understand you've made some headway in our mole situation."

"Well, our person, Quinn, at Perkins Klein has come up with more information on two companies you're currently bidding on."

"Really? Which ones?"

"Neotronix and Visionaire."

These are two companies with stiff competition to finance. Having them in our portfolio would further cement proof the mole isn't affecting us like the mole might like. "Shit. What do we do now?"

Jim explains an elaborate ruse he needs us to complete to possibly flush our mole out. I'm nervous yet confident that we may be seeing the light at the end of this tunnel. I'm ready to grow and not have to deal with the nonsense of a corporate spy in our midst.

Before we end the call, I ask, "Jim, one of the employees who's appeared on various lists as the mole has recently become very close to Mason. Do you have much on Annabel Ryan?"

I hear a computer clicking in the background, and then he tells me, "We did a lighter search of her. She's twenty-nine years old and lives in a shared apartment in the Marina. She has about $40,000 in debt between school loans and credit cards. No car. Her family lives in Southern California. She hasn't made any big purchases, and her bank account at the time had $600 in savings."

"I would be surprised if I was alone on this, but I'd like a super deep dive done on her. Like I mentioned, she seems to have wormed her way into a relationship with Mason that has the hair on the back of my neck standing on end."

"No problem. I'll keep you posted on what I find out on Sunday."

I immerse myself in my e-mail and try to get caught up. At six, Sara stops by and asks, "Care to join a few of us for a drink about eight at the bar across the street?"

"Sounds good. I'll meet you by the elevators."

I wonder how I can convince Hadlee to join us without being too obvious. I haven't called her since I got back, but I can't come up with a reason that doesn't sound like anything more than a booty call.

A more contrived reason to get together would be ideal.

Mason, Annabel, Sarah, and her fiancée, Trey, join us. Since Annabel hasn't adequately been vetted by Jim and his team, I'm not comfortable discussing much work-related progress, so we talk mostly about my ride home from the wedding and a bit of the trouble I found on my trip. Annabel is visibly bored by the conversation, and she whines to Mason. "Do you think we could head home? I'm exhausted."

Turning a slight shade of pink, he kisses her on the top of her head. "Sure."

After Mason finished business school, he kept telling us how to run our personal finances, so we usually stick him with the bill. Since he was convinced he was doing it so much better, he got to pay. He's always a good sport about it, but when he reaches for the check this time, I hold my hands up and say, "My turn. I've got this."

He nods at me, and he and Annabel leave. I watch how she grabs his hand and seems upset with him.

The three of us make small talk for a little longer when Trey finally says, "Well, since you two aren't going to bring up the elephant in the room, I will. What the fuck is Mason thinking?"

Sara shushes him. "We don't pass judgment on anyone's love life."

"Oh yes we do," I chime in. "I asked Jim to do a deep dive on her for Sunday night. But how are you doing? She's your admin."

"I'm not happy, but he's the managing partner. What can I say or do?"

"Sara, you're a partner. You can absolutely tell him to stop thinking with his Johnson and think with his head."

"When are Dillon and Emerson due back?" Sara asks.

Trey laughs. "If you're trying to change the subject, that won't work."

Shaking her head vehemently, she assures us, "Not at all. I'd like their perspective before we jump all over Mason."

She has a point. This should be a decision by all the partners, including Emerson and Dillon. "Okay, I'll buy into that. They're back next week, but I'm not exactly sure when. Let's also get feedback from Jim before we do anything."

SITTING IN OUR SUNDAY EVENING MEETING at Charles Arnaut's home, we have a fun group dinner prior to sitting as the management team in his office. Mason brought Annabel with him, and it makes some of the dinner conversation awkward. When we retire to Charles's office, Annabel attempts to join us, but Charles politely says, "Annabel, this is a partners meeting.

Margo would be happy to spend time with you while you wait for us."

She seems disappointed, which makes me a little happy. "Oh, okay."

"It's okay, Charles. She can join us," Mason interjects.

"Actually, no she can't. It's against our bylaws."

Thank God Charles agrees with us about Annabel.

"I forgot." Turning to Annabel, Mason says, "Sorry, sweetheart."

She gives him a deep kiss. "Don't worry about it. I probably would've been bored anyway. I'll ask if Margo would like some help cleaning up."

Charles pours an after-dinner drink for all of us while Jim starts the meeting with his review of Annabel. "She has about five thousand dollars in savings. We're chasing the increase over the last few months. Her debt has also increased slightly. We put a tail on her, but she goes home each night with Mason. They don't stay at her apartment."

Mason is bright red with anger. "Why the fuck are you investigating my girlfriend?"

"Mason, Annabel joined us shortly before the mole started their work," Sara explains. "She was also very determined to get involved with you. We need to protect ourselves. We did the same with each of us. She could be privy to all our inside information, and we need to be cautious."

Sara says it so much better than I ever could have. I would've been much more direct and probably only convinced him to propose or some shit and drive a wedge in our friendship.

"I've shared all sorts of things with her and trust her completely," Mason sneers.

"What have you shared?" Jim asks.

"These meetings, for example. And that we're hunting for a mole."

"Have you told her we have someone in place at Perkins Klein?"

"No." He stops and seems to be thinking about his answer. "Wait, I don't think so."

"You need to remember," Jim insists.

"I remember that when I told her about the mole, she was surprised and asked what we were doing. I told her we had several activities going."

What the fuck? This is pretty serious. What is he thinking?

No blow job, no matter how spectacular, is worth jeopardizing the company we've all put our heart and soul into building. I want to reach across and shake him to make him understand.

Breathe. In... out....

Charles is obviously unhappy. "Mason, anything discussed in a partners meeting is not to be discussed outside of this group. Not with your mother, your brother, your best friend, and most certainly not with your girlfriend."

"She's a sweet girl. I trust her," Mason repeats.

What the fuck? You trust her? No one else trusts her. Why can't you think with your head instead of your dick? I swear you are not thinking with the right head right now.

In... out....

Jim patiently says, "You can't trust anyone in a situation like this."

I want to kiss Jim. If Mason won't listen to me, maybe he'll listen to Charles and Jim.

"We got our acceptance from Cynthia Hathaway for the Business Development role. She's buying into a partnership. Does that mean we can't trust her either?" Mason says dejectedly.

That's good news, at least. I liked Cynthia and thought during the interview process that she would add value to the company very quickly.

"No. She was vetted, and background checked extensively. We can trust her."

"So was Annabel, and she's been with the company for over three years," Mason replies bitterly. "Plus, as part of the legal team, she has access to even more information with everything that crosses Sara's desk."

Jim and Charles exchange looks of apprehension. Mason clearly doesn't understand everyone's concern. She has him whipped. Where's my friend? He's usually the first one on alert when it comes to the health of our firm.

We can all tell that Mason's struggling with this. Charles carefully says, "Mason, I get that questioning your girlfriend's devotion may seem like an attack, and I would feel the same way if someone did that with my wife or kids, but please understand that we need to feel confident that what we say and do stays within our inner circle. We recognize Annabel will be ostracized by others at work because of her relationship with you. She may say things inadvertently and put all our work in jeopardy, which could take us back to square one with our hunt."

"Okay. I'm not happy, but I understand." Staring at each of us, he impresses, "But I trust Annabel, and I think you can, too."

I definitely don't think I can trust her. She's been on my list since I first made it. She was always there, listening and working in the background. The perfect cover for the mole.

Our meeting moves on to where things are with capturing information from some of Charles's friends.

As I drive back into the city later that night, I'm comforted to know that I'm not the only one whose radar is up on Annabel. I've known Mason for over fifteen years. He has always been the responsible one. I've been pegged as the irresponsible of the three of us. Annabel may be a nice girl, but she isn't the right person for him. She wants to be in the limelight and doesn't seem to want to share the attention. Mason is a self-made billionaire. He is the business behind our firm.

I wouldn't mind talking to Hadlee and getting her perspective on the situation. I got the impression that she isn't too fond of Annabel either.

chapter NINE

HADLEE

IT IS A CRAZY MONDAY. I had twenty-five patients on my schedule when I looked early this morning, and the phones hadn't even been turned on for those needing same-day sick visits.

My cell phone rings and I'm not familiar with the number. Rather than answer the call, I walk in to see a patient.

We're just getting started when my medical assistant knocks on the door. "Dr. Hadlee, there's an emergency. Can you please step out a moment?"

Apologizing to my patient, I step out and ask, "Is everything okay? Have we called 911?"

Maria is clearly nervous, wringing her hands. That isn't normal. We have the occasional issue in the office when a child has a severe asthma attack or maybe an epileptic seizure, but she's rarely this bad. "Dr. Hadlee, your tenant called. Your house is on fire, and the fire department is trying to put the fire out."

I freeze. My stomach drops to the floor, and I find it difficult to breathe as her words finally register. *Fire? How can that be?* "What? What do you mean?"

"I've called you a Lyft." Glancing at her phone, she says, "They're two minutes out." She leads me to my office and guides me to put my computer away, helps me remove my lab coat, and finally picks up my purse and walks me outside to the waiting car. I'm in complete shock. *Fire? How did that happen? Did I turn the stove off this morning after I made my breakfast? I'm sure I did.* I don't hear anything she's saying to me until "Dr. Kim will cover your patients. Go home and take care of yourself."

"I don't understand. How did the fire start?"

She pushes me into the waiting ride share and tells them, "Put a rush on it."

The drive home passes in a blur: no traffic lights, no turning from one street to another, not even parking outside the yellow tape. The entire block is like something out of a horror movie, a ball of black smoke and red, white, and orange flames stretching from the broken windows and roof. The firefighters flooding homes with water from ladders and the street. There won't be anything to salvage, not a damn thing. The air smells of burning, acrid, chemical-infused and choking. My eyes move from face to face in the gathering crowd, then water. I'm at a loss. What do I do? I stand here paralyzed.

I spot my tenant. She has a blanket wrapped around her and looks disheveled, and I can see dried tears that have carved out the black ash on her face. I run up to her and we embrace. "Michelle? Are you, all right?"

She looks at me. "Yes. I'm fine. I smelled the fire and then saw smoke. I called 911 and then your office. It didn't start in your house."

"All that matters is that we're fine."

"Hadlee, you've been a great landlord, and the first floor flat in your home was great, but I think this is a higher power telling me it's time to move home to Minneapolis."

I'm not surprised by this. Michelle came out here chasing a boy, and when it didn't work out, she floundered and has struggled ever since. "I understand. I don't know what my insurance will pick up, but find a hotel and a place to spend the night. You can bill me."

"Thanks." She begins to cry again. "I booked a flight home from my cell phone for tomorrow morning. I don't think I'll be back, but I'll keep in touch."

I can't help but panic a moment. Michelle was in this with me, and now she's heading home fifteen hundred miles away. I'm not prepared for this and everything it means. "What will I do with your things?"

Smearing the ash from her face, she pulls the blanket tighter around her. "I don't think there's anything left."

I count eight fire trucks, and dozens of firefighters working to put the fire out. It's controlled chaos. Fire hoses line the black streets like giant beige veins pumping water from the ground and the trucks. I cry quietly from behind the yellow tape street. I watch the news trucks filming and all the people watching as the block burns, and because of the proximity, the entire block of homes seem to be burning, too. but when I lift the tape to walk closer, a police officer stops me. "Ma'am, you can't cross the line."

Crying, I sniff out, "I received a call, and I've been told my house is burning. What do I do?"

"What's your address?"

It rolls off my tongue without a second thought. I'm hoping

it really is just a dream, and everything I own isn't gone.

He lifts the yellow tape and ushers me inside. "Please, right this way."

My heart breaks as he motions over an official-looking person who walks me behind a firetruck. "Hello, I'm Captain Whalley. I understand your house is one of these on the street?"

The snapping of wood surrounds me as fire flickers, flares, leaps, and spits, showering sparks like a fountain. Plumes of black smoke wind around the homes like great hungry snakes, devouring everything in its path. Choking clouds of noxious smoke, inferno, blazing, out of control, ash floating to the ground like great dirty flakes of snow, showering onto everything, sprinkling onto the ground. "Yes," I whisper, trying to take in all the activity. "What happened?"

"It seems your next-door neighbor had an electrical short. Unfortunately, the fire spread to your home and four others. Theirs is completely destroyed, but we're trying to save yours and the rest of the block."

"What do I do?"

He puts his arm around me. "Do you have a boyfriend or a good friend you can call?"

I nod, standing frozen watching the fire, unable to do anything or make any calls.

Before I can figure it out, I hear my name being called by a familiar voice. "Hadlee!"

I break into tears when my eyes meet CeCe's.

She talks to the officer on duty, who allows her to pass, and she runs over. "Maria got my number from your computer and told me what was happening. Are you okay?"

I nod at her numbly, and she stands with me as the fire moves to two more homes and four more firetrucks arrive. We stand for a what seems like forever. I'm paralyzed by watching all the activity. I have the urge to run in and grab anything that may not have burned, but it's too late. My house is black smoke and orange flames.

CeCe stands with me valiantly, and we watch the choreographed dance the firemen do, holding the fire to only a few homes. I don't realize she's left my side until she places a blanket around my shoulders to keep me warm.

In the dark smoke, orange flames have blown out the windows, sending horizontal jets of flame out ten feet or more. I can feel the radiating heat on my face from across the street. The firefighters can only watch it burn and try their best protect my house, spraying foam on the sides and roof.

I'm exhausted and ready to collapse. "Miss Ford?"

I look up but don't really see the man standing in front of me.

When I can't string two words together, CeCe answers, "She's Dr. Ford. Is there any news?"

He puts his hand on my arm. "I'm sorry about your home. You won't be able to get into the house today. Is there a number you can leave with us? We'll want to speak with you, probably tomorrow."

CeCe leaves her number with someone and explains she's taking me to her house if they have any questions.

When she ushers me to her car, I notice the parking ticket. "Damn those parking enforcement asses," CeCe rages.

Reaching for the ticket, I say, "I'll take care of it."

"Oh no, you won't. I chose to park here to get to you quickly. I knew I was partially in the crosswalk."

I'm still stunned by everything I've seen. "I don't know what to do."

"Do you have your insurance broker's number?"

"No, and I don't know my policy number, either."

"Don't worry. We have Google and we'll find them. Your insurance broker should have your policy number and will take care of you. That's why we have insurance. Now let's get you to my place. We'll get you a bath and something to eat."

"Okay." I stare out the passenger side window, not listening to what CeCe is saying into her phone as we return to her house. All the things I can't replace that were in my house come to me in bits and pieces: pictures of my parents, my mother's engagement ring, my grandmother's pearls, my original diplomas, my passport, and essentially all my clothes. I'm so overwhelmed by everything that I can't move.

CeCe parks her car and walks me to her condo, heading directly to the master bathroom and her Jacuzzi tub. Running me a hot bath, she helps me get undressed. I'm so overcome with grief, I can't even remember the simplest things. The last time I felt this way was when my dad told me my mother had died.

I sit in the bathtub until the water is cold and my fingers are turning blue. CeCe's called in reinforcements and helps me dress before they arrive. Sara, Trey, and Greer all appear before I know it, bearing flowers, dinner, wine, and lots of encouragement. We're all sitting around the living room. They're eating and trying to bring me into the conversations, but I'm numb.

I don't hear the doorbell ring, but CeCe gets up and opens

the door, and a woman walks in with six giant bags from Nordstrom's. "Jennifer. Thank you so much for coming to help my friend out."

Turning to me, Jennifer says, "Come join me in the bedroom. Let's see what I've brought and make sure it fits."

My medical school loans are close to $300,000. What was left of my trust fund, I put into the down payment on the house. I could only make my mortgage payment with a tenant in the downstairs flat. Now with the fire, I won't be able to do that. I whisper to her, "I can't afford this."

Patting me on the arm, she says, "Please don't worry about it. You're all covered."

I cry at the generosity of my good friend CeCe. We've been friends since we started kindergarten together. After my mother died, each of my father's subsequent seven wives took more and more of his money, the last leaving me with barely $200,000. My financial planner suggested the house, and now I have nothing. Not to mention, everything my mother left me was in the house. I cry deep and heavy sobs.

CeCe slips into the room. "Honey, let me help you. I gave her the sizes we talked about at the wedding. Some may be too big, and if so, it's all my fault."

Jennifer reaches out and says, "Let's start with undergarments." Standing, she opens a bag with an assortment of beautiful panties and matching bras. CeCe pats me on the arm. "Honey, let this be my treat."

Between the sobs, I cry, "I can't. This is far too generous."

"If you insist, you can pay me back later once you get your insurance check and replace your more important things." She pulls me in close and gives me a comforting hug. "You have insurance. We'll get this all figured out. Meanwhile, you need clothes. The jeans you were wearing are filthy and smell like smoke. We may have to throw them out."

"I'll pay you back. You're not my bank," I tell her as Jennifer begins pulling items out of a bag.

"Here, put these beautiful panties on." Searching through several bags, she says, "Here's a nice pair of pajamas. I think these are modest enough that you can wear them with everyone outside."

Jeans, shirts, clothes for work, clothes for going out—plenty for me to wear. I'm stunned at how quickly Jennifer pulled everything together so accurately to my size and needs.

The cloud begins to lift. My friends have been helpful and nurturing. Bad news spreads quickly, but I'm incredibly grateful that my cell phone is full of messages from friends and my office. I return the most pressing calls before I collapse and fall asleep in CeCe's guest room. CeCe gets me a small sleeping pill, but my sleep is not restful. I dream of the fire. I dream of my last stepmother, who laughs at as she tells me how she's spent all my dad's money, leaving me without any inheritance. I keep thinking about my house and everything I've lost. I go through a list of what I'll need to replace. Some things were insured, but the pictures of my mom are gone, along with everything I have of her. The loss of the connection to my mom sends me into a downward spiral. I cry while holding the pillow, wishing for someone to hold me and comfort me.

CeCe knocks on my door. "Hadlee?"

I roll over and notice it's after nine. It may not have been restful, but I did get some sleep. "Come in."

Opening the door, she has a fragrant cup of coffee that she hands to me. "Hey, sleepyhead. How did you sleep?"

"Not great."

"I'm sorry I woke you. The fire department called, and they'd like to meet you at the house this morning. Should I call them and let them know you aren't able to make it?"

"No. I can hop in the shower, get dressed, and grab a Lyft. My car is still at my office."

"I'll take you. I've taken the day off and will help however I can."

Dressed in a new pair of jeans and a white designer T-shirt, I climb in CeCe's car and we head over to the house. My distinctive Victorian seems fine from the front if you look very closely and notice the gray hue or the hole in the roof and the sky that can be seen through the front windows. The charred remains of my house break my heart. It was so alive, so vibrant prior to the fire. Inside had been a place of love and security, a place with memories and warmth. Now the wind whistles through, the steady rain falling right into the twisted plastic and metal that had been furniture and electronics. In those ashes lie my photographs, my art, all my personal possessions.

The fire marshal meets me with a large box. "I think your bedroom is relatively okay. There'll be some smoke damage, but it's dry. The wall at the back of your closet protected much of your bedroom, and the bedroom door was closed before the smoke and fire could ruin too much. The fire started in the back corner, and your bedroom was street facing. That helped a lot. We put what we could in the box. I'm sorry it isn't more."

My hand goes to my mouth, and I begin to cry again. That's

where I kept many of the things I have from my mother. I peek in the box and spot the photos I treasure most, plus my jewelry box. "Thank you. Thank you so very much."

CeCe wraps her arms around my shoulders. "When can we have access so we can move some things into storage?"

"We're watching for hot spots right now, but I would think by tomorrow it should be okay. For now, there's a police officer 24/7 to make sure there are no looters. But I must warn you, there are things in the bathroom and the bedrooms, though much of it isn't worth saving with all the smoke damage."

"We understand. We can come back," CeCe assures him.

The sun shows me the six homes affected; my home in the middle sustained quite a bit of damage. "I was told they think it was an electrical fire in my next-door neighbor's home?"

"That's what the fire investigator believes. A lot of these prewar homes have tube and knob wires hidden in the walls."

I nod. "When I bought the house three years ago, I ripped all the tube and knob out and had it rewired. It was costly but worth it. I guess it didn't matter in the end."

"I wouldn't say that. She was lucky her house didn't go up years ago, and you won't have to completely tear down to rebuild. The city doesn't make it easy with homes of your age."

As we walk to CeCe's car, she says, "It seems we have a full day today, but we can't do it on an empty stomach. Let's go find some breakfast."

I nod and run through my mental checklist of everything I have to do, trying not to hyperventilate the longer it gets. I can't stay at CeCe's. I love her, and her friendship means so much to me, but we don't live well together. I'm too much of a slob, and my work schedule is hard on her. Though my initial conversation with the insurance broker didn't seem to indicate I had any rental coverage, which leaves me few options.

Over breakfast, CeCe gets out a pad of paper and pen from her purse, and together we work on my list. I need to call my lender and make them aware of what happened. Essentially the bank owns the bulk of the house since I still have over twenty-five years on the mortgage. Plus calling the gas and electric company, water company, and cable company. Not to mention I have to figure out what to do with my car. It can't stay parked at the office. CeCe takes half the list and promises she's going to take care of it, including getting packing materials and a storage unit for what we can salvage and any replacements we buy.

I spend the afternoon talking to insurance, my lender, and my office. The insurance company is expecting my neighbor's coverage to cover it. I explained that she says she doesn't have coverage, but until they get that from official channels, they aren't going to do anything. The good news is the lender is only asking for interest payments—which isn't necessarily a huge break, but I can make that without my rental income. I feel bad that I've left my teammates at work hanging, but they understand.

By the end of the day, I'm exhausted, but I feel like I got a few things accomplished.

chapter
TEN

CAMERON

IT'S BEEN ONE OF THOSE DAYS, and I'm exhausted. I'm grateful Dillon and Emerson have returned from their honeymoon in Greece. They seem so refreshed. To celebrate, we've all agreed to meet for a nice dinner to hear about their trip. The G-rated version, I hope.

"Hey, man, it's great to have you home," I tell Dillon.

Emerson leans over to Sara and ask, "Okay, what's going on with Mason and Annabel? We were surprised too when she showed up at the wedding."

"I guess they're getting serious." Tears pool in Sarah's eyes.

"Are you kidding?"

"Unfortunately I'm not. Cameron's insisted that Jim and his team do a more thorough background check. It has Mason rather upset," Sara tells Emerson.

"Dillon is fit to be tied. Not only does it open us up to a sexual harassment suit, but because we're at risk with the mole, he doesn't want anyone in the company brought into the inner circle."

I'm relieved to hear that I'm not the only one who thinks the affair with Annabel is a train wreck waiting to happen on so many levels.

As we take our seats at the table, I sit next to Hadlee. I have her panties from Breckenridge in my pocket. I'd planned to return them and ask for a repeat, but Hadlee's not interested in speaking to me at all right now. I guess I'm in the doghouse already. I'm not very good when it comes to relationships. My parents were never role models, and whenever I've been serious with a girl, I've found a way to not only fuck it up to where she doesn't just leave me, she goes away mad.

Turning to me after the first course, Hadlee shares, "I'm sorry, Cameron. I'm terribly distracted and awful company. My house recently had a fire, and I spoke with the insurance company today."

Holy crap! That's awful. "Your house burned? Were you hurt?"

"I was at work. My first-floor tenant called the fire department. It happened last week. The fire took most of the homes on the block on my side of the street."

"Oh, I saw that in *The Chronicle.* It was an electrical fire, right?" She nods at me. "Did the fire start in your place?" The paper made it sound very tragic. I guess there were six homes involved, which affected over thirty people. I'm glad she's okay.

"No, it started next door, and she doesn't have the insurance to cover the loss of my house or the others. My insurance company is giving me a hard time, but I have the things that mean the most to me. CeCe helped me move what little was salvageable into storage, and the fire department delivered a box of what they were able to get out of my bedroom. I only care that I have pictures of my mom and a few mementos. She died when I was nine."

I didn't know she lost her mom at a young age, too. Something we have in common. "I lost mine at twelve. She was in a car accident with a drunk driver. I don't know what I would do if I lost the few things I have to remember her by."

"I'm so sorry. That must've been awful for you. So sudden. My mom died of breast cancer, and it was fast, but I felt like I got to say goodbye."

Her eyes glass over, and I can tell it's still an emotional pull for her. "I'm sure that must've been hard. My dad never remarried. How about yours?"

"I wish I could say the same. My father remarried seven more times. My last step-monster spent all the money my mother left me when she died."

"That's rough."

Her lips curve despite the tragedy of growing up without her mother and the recent fire. "Honestly, I couldn't care less about the money, but it upsets me that she spent it on things she'll be giving to her own kids."

"Can you do anything about it?"

"Probably, but every lawyer I've ever spoken to has said it would cost hundreds of thousands of dollars to fight it. It honestly doesn't mean that much to me."

I'm stunned by the revelation. I knew Hadlee had grown up with CeCe. Her grandfather founded a large high-end hotel chain, and I always assumed she was an heiress to a fortune and as monied as the Arnaults were. It's refreshing to have someone in our circle who's so grounded and unaffected by money.

"When is the builder telling you he can get you back into your place?"

"I can't find anyone to talk to me until the insurance company decides what they're going to do. I've had several offers to buy the land, and they'll clear it and deal with the city's building codes nightmare, but they're giving me less than what I owe on the house, so it's overwhelming. I still have undergrad and medical school loans."

"The paper made it sound like there were several homes affected. I'm sorry yours was one of them. Where are you going to live?"

"I'm considering a studio in the Tenderloin district."

"Are you kidding? You'll be fighting with the homeless and the drug addicts outside your door, not to mention possibly in your hallways. You can't live there. It's not safe." I'm not sure where my protective side is coming from. If anyone else were to tell me they wanted to live in the slums of the Tenderloin, I would say, "Good for you." But I can see how vulnerable Hadlee is right now, and I want to protect her.

She smiles at me and puts her hand on my arm. "I can't live in CeCe's guest room forever. I think she's ready to have her place back to herself."

I have a downstairs executive rental in my house which is empty, and my accountant would prefer I not rent it out because it's more income that negatively impacts my taxes. "Hadlee, my tenant recently moved out of my downstairs apartment. It's a two-bedroom place on the first floor."

"Thank you, but I don't have any furniture."

I can't let her go to an apartment in the Tenderloin district. It isn't safe. That isn't a problem. "It's an executive rental, so it's furnished. You can stay as long as you need to. You have your own entrance and plenty of privacy. When you move out, I'll either rent it as an executive rental again, or maybe make it an Airbnb." I'm not sure where my offer came from. She looks as shocked as I feel. It would be great to see her more often, but it probably means that I won't be able to sleep with her. Technically, she'd be living under my roof, and that could make things very awkward.

"I'd hate to take money out of your pocket by occupying the apartment. I don't know...."

Before she can turn me down, I try one more time. "My accountant would prefer I not have any rental income, but the house is too big for just me. You can stay for free, or if it makes you feel better, you can rent it for, say, two hundred dollars. Why don't you bring CeCe by tomorrow and you can check it out? I'm in Pacific Heights." I'm trying to be a nice guy, and I feel like I need to talk her into this. Why am I trying so hard? If she doesn't want to see me again, I need to just let it go, but I can't seem to.

CeCe must've overheard the end of the conversation, because she chimes in at that point. "We'll be there. Text me your home address and we'll stop by around seven, okay?"

chapter ELEVEN

HADLEE

I CAN'T BELIEVE I AGREED to check out Cameron's place. I want to explore something with him, but I can't if I'm living as his tenant. Plus, I'm a mess right now.

At least he's wonderful to look out for me. CeCe was very clear that she didn't want me living in the Tenderloin, but it was all I can afford. I still have a mortgage to make and I've lost my rental income, plus my school loans are the size of a mortgage payment too. She insists I can stay at her place, but there was no way I'm going to allow her to continue to pay for me, and besides, we don't live under the same roof well. We tried that when I was struggling with my third stepmother, and it didn't work out well. Our friendship is much too important to risk. Growing up, she included me on family vacations, and she was the constant source of mental stability for me after my mom died. All of the Arnaults were wonderful when everything was crazy with my father and the rotation of stepmothers. They're my family.

As the Lyft drops us in front of Cameron's home, I note that the house is identical to its neighbors right down to the shade of paint on the iron balconies. But I can tell which one belongs to him right away. Whereas every other dwelling is simply towering red brick, his motorcycle is sitting out front and hard to miss. It's a badass bike, that's for sure. All I know is it's a Harley, and it looks expensive.

Without even checking the number on the door, we rap the brass lion knocker three times and wait. In a brief lull of the San Francisco traffic, I hear his approaching footfalls. The door opens, and I'm momentarily stunned by the wifebeater stretched across his broad chest, the low-hanging faded jeans, and the incredible tattoos. My heart beats faster, and my panties dampen from the memory of what he's capable of. I want to get on my knees and beg him to take me.

"Cameron, I had no idea you were sleeved in tattoos," CeCe exlaims. She reaches out to run her fingers on his arm. "They're so beautiful."

"Thank you. It's a dragon that wraps around my entire torso and arms. It's a symbol of how alcoholism destroys everything in its wake. It's taken a while to finish, but I have a great artist I work with on Folsom Street."

"I can tell. It's stunning. I don't think there's anything I like today that I would like five years from now, let alone for the rest of my life. Your artwork is so impressive."

"My mother was killed by a drunk driver when I was twelve."

"Oh, I'm so sorry. What a tragedy to lose your mother at such a young age. You and Hadlee have that in common."

"Yes, we've talked about it." He steps outside and beckons us to follow him. "The apartment has its own entrance. We do share the laundry room and have access via separate doors, but I promise I'll never enter your space unless invited." He hardly looks at me. Seems like there's no option for round two with him.

He opens the door and motions us in. We walk along a wide hallway, and it opens to a bright and cheery living area. He shows us the laundry room off in the corner, painted yellow with a high-end front-loading washer and dryer, drying racks, and tables at a perfect height for folding.

He points to a door on the opposite side. "If you lock your side, I won't have access."

"Great idea."

"As I said, the apartment is set up as an executive rental, so it's fully furnished."

I slowly glance around, everything well decorated with a perfect balance of symmetry, color, and fashion in every part of each room. It appears neither masculine nor feminine but a balance of both. Everything seems neat, clean and fresh, including the soft comforter to wrap around my body. The kitchen is full of high-end appliances, and I'm stunned at how beautiful it is. It's nicer than my own home.

Cameron presents me with a Nespresso, and we all stand in the backyard garden and take in the view of the Golden Gate Bridge.

"Wow. This is quite the view," I exclaim.

"Thank you. I should use this patio more often. I always seem to want to when I have someone living in the apartment, but I don't want to intrude." Staring at me intently, he asks, "What do you think?"

"It's beautiful. But I think you'll be losing too much money to rent it to me at such a low rate."

"Actually, you'll be doing me a favor. I believe I told you my accountant has been after me about not renting it. With it being an executive, it's paid the entire mortgage on the house for the last nine months. If you live here the next six months or even a year, it helps give me the write-off I need. Plus I know you well enough to know you'll take good care of the place, and I'm not here alone."

This would be so much better than staying in the fleabag studio apartment I visited last week. The apartment manager seemed a little shifty, but I figured I could manage it for a few months. It's positively beautiful, and I might get an excuse to hang out with him, even if sleeping with the landlord is a bad idea. "I would take very good care of your place. It's very tempting."

"Great. When do you want to move in?"

"Well, I do have a lot of things. I'll need to arrange for packers and movers." I swear his jaw drops. It's fun to give him a hard time. "I'm kidding. I don't even have a suitcase, but I can buy a few big black trash bags and two boxes of stuff they salvaged from my house to move over."

"You will not! I have a suitcase, and we can get you a few nicer boxes from work."

"All right then, I guess that means I can move in at your convenience."

Taking a key from his pocket, he places it in my hand. My heart beats faster as an electric current pulsates through his touch.

This may be a bad idea.

Two days later, I'm in the middle of unpacking when I hear a knock at my front door. I wasn't expecting anyone and haven't given anyone my new address. Peeking through the peephole, I see it's Cameron.

Opening the door, I brush my auburn hair behind my ear and grin widely. He has a large white paper bag, and it smells amazing. "I thought I would bring you some dinner. It's Greek. I hope you like Greek food."

"I love anything I don't have to cook."

He helps me set the table and says, "It'll be great to have a woman living here for a change."

"You don't rent to women?"

"Not on purpose. I use an agency, and they seem to rent to high-powered men. Maybe only men rent executive rentals? I don't know."

We enjoy our dinner, and it's comfortable and fun. As the evening comes to a close, he says, "Oh, I almost forgot." Standing, he takes out a pair of lacey panties from his pocket. "I thought you might like these back."

Blushing from head to toe, I tell him, "Thanks. I searched everywhere for these that morning but couldn't find them. Where were they?"

"I put them in my coat pocket when I removed them. I think, at least subconsciously, I wanted a repeat of our evening."

"But you don't anymore?"

I can't tell if he's looking at with me pity or disappointment. "Hadlee, I do, but right now you're too vulnerable, and if we choose to go along that path again, we need to have a good conversation about it first."

"A conversation? Well I'm disease free. Not only do I get checked annually for work, but I have an IUD, and I haven't been with anyone for almost year before we were together."

He seems shocked by my revelation. "Okay, but you're still homeless, and I don't want you to ever feel like I'm taking advantage of you."

We sit in silence, and I come to realize that he wants it as bad as I do. It's a start.

Getting up from the table, he kisses me on the forehead. "Sleep well, and if you need anything, please don't hesitate to call."

As I lie in bed a little while later, I relive our conversation over and over.

What did he mean by saying he wants a conversation before he'll sleep with me again? Why do guys talk in code?

chapter TWELVE

CAMERON

I'M SITTING IN MY OFFICE when my admin comes in. "Mason has asked the partners to meet in his office in ten minutes."

I'm completely immersed in these lines of code to find a mistake—unsuccessfully, of course. I didn't hear exactly what she said, so I just stare at her. "What?"

Frustrated by my not paying attention, she speaks louder. "Mason wants you in his office in ten minutes."

"Did he say why?" I have a lot to get done, and I've been a bit distracted knowing I have a beautiful woman at my house.

She has a look of annoyance that says, "Just go to the meeting and leave me to my job."

"Never mind. Ten minutes. I'll be there," I tell her.

I can't find the mistake. It's so frustrating. E-mailing the code to a member of my team, I request, Something's off. Can you find it? I then get up with my coffee cup in hand and head over to the kitchen where I run into Dillon.

"Do you have any idea what's going on?" I ask.

"No, man. Do you?"

I shake my head and pour myself a large cup of coffee, doctoring it with cream and sugar. We talk about the 49ers' football expectations. The company has season tickets, and these last few years it's been tough to get people to go to games. "We need to upgrade to a box."

"I agree, but that's a pretty hefty chunk of change, and these days we can't always give tickets away if they can't at least win 50 percent of their games."

Sitting in Mason's office, we wait for him to join us. It's Cynthia Hathaway's first day of work, and we're taking her to lunch. She's a new partner and head of Business Development. We stole her from a smaller competitor who recently went under, and she has an amazing reputation in The Valley with many of the who's who.

When we hired Cynthia, she was put through a much deeper background check than any other partner had been through. She was two years behind me at Stanford and has a firm grasp on technology. She'll be a nice counterpoint to Dillon when it comes to convincing people with great ideas to only take our money.

Emerson has Cynthia's first week of work planned already. I spend time with her tomorrow, or maybe it's Thursday. When she walks into the room, I'm impressed. Cynthia's wearing a pair of tight jeans, boots to her knees with a huge platform heel that makes her close in height to Sara and Emerson, a floral print blouse, and a suede chocolate-colored coat. Her dark brown hair has subtle auburn highlights, and the color reminds me of Hadlee.

I wonder what she's doing right now.

Mason arrives with Sara on his heels. "Sorry, I was talking to

Jim on the encrypted phone—" He stops when he sees Cynthia. "Cynthia, welcome. Things aren't always this crazy."

Emerson leans over to her and says, "That's what they told me. Don't believe him. I've been here almost three years, and it's always this crazy." She gives Cynthia a reassuring smile.

"Well okay, it's always like this, but I'd like to move to a point where we're less reactive and more proactive." Glancing carefully around the group, Mason continues, "Jim called to tell me that Tom Perkins had a heart attack last night and is in critical condition at Palo Alto Memorial."

We all stop talking, and the few of us who were distracted by our cell phones are now listening with rapt attention. Tom is one of the founding partners of Perkins Klein, one of our biggest competitors. They've been winning a lot of the business we've been losing, which we've been attributing to the mole.

"That doesn't sound good," Dillon says.

"No, it doesn't," I agree.

Sara turns to Dillon and asks, "Do we have any financial models that speak to how this is going to affect them?"

"Honestly, no. I'm not one to go morbid in my models. I have one for if he were to leave, but that would mean he takes some of the investments, so they wouldn't apply." Dillon looks over at Sara. "How about legally?"

"Mason only told me a few minutes ago, but I think they'll lose a few deals that they may be close to closing that might be worth picking up. But I'm not sure of the financial repercussions. He's the main advisor to many of the companies they've invested in, and I can't imagine Terry Klein being able to cover all those companies. I think we need to reach out to Charles and get his thoughts. And of course, we need to know how things are internally from Quinn."

"I have calls in to Trey, CeCe, and Charles. Really, I think we need to get Cynthia and Dillon out and talking to people who were in their pipeline like they did to us when Dillon took his leave. Anyone else disagree?"

"No, I think that's wise," Emerson shares. "I'll also have my team put their ears to the ground. We might be able to make up some of the position we lost recently." Almost as an afterthought, she asks, "Could this mean our mole goes dormant?"

Sitting back, I add, "One can only hope."

Mason dismisses the team, and I walk back to my office. What would it mean if Perkins Klein were to fail? They're a huge organization. I've ridden my motorcycle with Tom, and he's young. We may be competitors, but outside of work, we're buddies. The idea that he could have a heart attack at such a young age is a little disconcerting. I could always eat better and work out more. They also say married men live longer, but that isn't in the cards for me, just like it isn't in the cards for him.

Women aren't crazy about my work schedule, and if I'm being honest, I don't know how to do relationships. With my last girlfriend, I was always in trouble for spending too much time at work. One day she'd complain I wasn't calling enough and the next I was calling too much. Really, she wanted someone who would open up and tell her their deepest, darkest secrets. I don't know how to do that. I don't know how to be vulnerable, she'd tell me. Truthfully, I'm not even vulnerable in the sex that I prefer. I'm sure I should spend time on a therapist's couch, but right now I don't have the time to spare.

My mind wanders back to Tom. We've been friends for a long time. I could always show up at his house unannounced. If something was bothering me, but I wasn't ready to talk about it, he'd offer me a beer and a spot on his couch, and then we'd hang out watching *Sports Center.* When I was ready, we'd talk about it. He always listened without judgment and never commented until I'd spun my heart out. Then he would put his beer aside, look me in the eyes, and give me advice like the brother I never had. He never mocked unless I needed a good kick in the butt, and he never told a soul even a hint of what we discussed. He's a black hole for gossip, a true friend, one of a kind.

Knowing Tom is less than ten years older than me and in decent shape puts me in a bit of a funk. As I get off my bike in my driveway, I watch Hadlee approach. She's a vision in jeans, sexy-as-hell sandals, and a green floral print blouse that sets off her eyes and hides her beautiful breasts behind a black leather jacket.

"We really ought to stop running into each other this way," she teases me, and I tip my hat with a happy grin.

"Where are you off to?"

"Meeting CeCe, Greer, and Emerson downtown for dinner. Would you like to join us?"

"It would certainly be more fun hanging out with the four of you than what I have planned, but I'll leave you to your girls' night out."

Her look immediately makes my cock hard. We talk for a few more moments until her ride arrives. She turns to stare at me and waves. "If you change your mind, text me. We'd love for you to join us."

Since I'm sure Hadlee is out, I grab a beer and make my way

downstairs to the patio, lighting a citronella candle at the center of the table and taking a seat to watch the traffic in the distance across the Golden Gate while I drink my beer. I feel drawn to her, but I know the darkness that lives within me is not what she deserves.

As the sun goes to rest, the moon takes its place and the darkness surrounds me. I like the night—it hides my flaws, my imperfections, the scars burned onto my flesh, the stab wounds the knives of my history left behind. The moon guides me through the night. I slowly close my eyes in her calming presence, my body quietly switching off, but she lets my soul run free. I can do the things I would never be allowed to do when the sun is out. I can do whatever I want, my worries, my thoughts silently burning up into smoke as they wander through the endless night once more.

I'm reminded of Hadlee's perfume sitting here in the garden. Clouding my vision, my mind drifts to the pure ecstasy on her face when she comes.

Caught up in a primal state of lust, I wait for her to return. I want her tonight. I want to feel her creamy skin beneath me. I want to taste her sweet musky core. I want to feel her constrict around my cock as she writhes in passion when she creams all over me. My heart beats fast, but I take a few deep breaths as I ask it to be calm.

I live for women who misbehave. I love the naughty ones. I wonder how Hadlee misbehaves in the bedroom, if she'll allow me to spank her. I daydream about a handprint on her ass. It may have only been one night, but my tongue knows every secret magic place on her body.

Taking a deep breath, I realize I've been sitting outside for too long. If she comes home and sees me here, I won't be able to control myself, and that'll create a whole new set of challenges.

chapter THIRTEEN

HADLEE

I'VE LIVED IN CAMERON'S PLACE for almost a full month now. I often hear his motorcycle when he arrives home late, or his footfalls above me. I want to call him and invite myself up, but I never do.

I'm surprised when I arrive home and Cameron is sitting on the back patio, watching the sunset as he nurses a beer. I pour myself a glass of wine and join him.

A blast of humid night air hits me when I open the door, in sharp contrast to the cool interior. I sit next to him on the patio with a glass of silky smooth merlot. I'm not sure what's going through his mind, but I'm preoccupied with my last appointment of the day, and the silence between us is welcomed.

I had to tell one of my favorite families that their daughter, Lilly, has leukemia. Kids don't deserve that. It's days like today that I hate my job. Yesterday was their last normal day. They could laugh and hope. I've now left a permanent mark on the family, one they'll never forget.

I set them up with a translator and two-dozen appointments with various doctors who'll make up their care team. Today there were understandably heartbroken. In a few weeks, the reality of what they're up against will sink in. Parents will feel uneasy about the terrible choices they'll have to make. They'll choose life-threatening treatments for a chance to save their child's life.

I'll still treat their other children, and we'll talk about the awful days of nonstop vomiting, the pain in their child's eyes when they witness her hair fall out, the ache of loneliness they feel from isolation due to compromised immune systems. We'll talk about crying in the shower so their children won't hear them because they feel so helpless, and we'll whisper to one another the fear we have that their beautiful little girl might die.

I experience guilt every time I learn of such an awful diagnosis, another child's relapse, another child who has died from cancer or a side effect of treatment. Every. Time.

Sitting outside, my mind races with everything that happened today and I'm numb. I want to feel something. Watching Cameron, I notice something seems to be bothering him, too. I don't want to be alone tonight. I reach for Cameron's hand, surprised to find I'm nervous. I know I affect him. I can see the impact when we're alone together. And I watch how much he fights it. But tonight, he seems completely unaffected, his expression stern as I sit next to him with my glass. I drain it quickly, partially to make up for the shitty day I had and partially for the courage.

He stares at me. "Rough day?"

I take a big breath and close my eyes, hoping he can hear the need in my voice. "Please fuck me."

I open my eyes and gaze at the conflict in his, but I know he wants this as bad as I do. "I want to be clear, Hadlee. I absolutely fuck. There is no making love. I like it hard and rough. Do you think you can manage that tonight?"

I nod and whisper, "I need you."

In less than two seconds, he has us standing, his hands tangled in my hair as his lips come crashing down on mine. His hands are rough, and I love that he's taking me away from the pain of my day.

I open my mouth to him, and he responds immediately by slipping his tongue past my lips. When our tongues touch, it feels as if I'm being zapped with a thousand watts of electricity. It's as I remember—hot, raw, and aggressive. My pulse increases, and I arch my back and press my breasts into him, showing they're aching to be caressed, licked, and sucked. He growls against my lips in appreciation of what my body is doing all on its own.

He pressed into me, and I feel the rhythmic beat inside his chest. He fits so well with me, including his cock that he nestles at the apex of my thighs. I'm under an attack of the most erotic kind, and the last nail in my coffin is when I catch the faint aroma of his sweat mixed with his sandalwood scent.

He removes my shirt and quickly unclasps my bra, then pinches and pulls at my nipples. His engorged cock pushes at my stomach, and my body clenches from the rush of excitement. I reach for his hard cock, his small moans as he aggressively kisses me spurring me on. I pull the cushion from the chair and get on my knees in front of him, then peel his jeans and boxers off him. Our eyes lock as he watches me slowly lick the tip of his cock, tasting his precum. He draws in a deep breath as I lick the entire length, completely wetting it so I can stroke it with some friction while I suck each of his balls.

"Oh, Hadlee," he hisses.

I place my thumb at the base of his cock and work it in small circles, taking his cock deep in my throat. He pushes in even deeper, until I'm not sure how much more I can take. My core is aching and in need of his magic touch, but I keep going, sucking him into my mouth.

"I want to come while inside you." Grabbing me by the hand, he leads me to his bedroom. "Take your clothes off," he demands.

I glance at him and sway to an invisible beat as I pull at my nipples. I stretch my tongue and carefully lick the tip of one nipple. He's memorized, staring straight at me, barely breathing.

I turn around as I unbutton my pants, inching them over my hips and pulling my panties over my ass, giving him a clear look. I step out of my sandals and begin to remove my pants when I hear him growl, "Put your shoes back on."

I turn and ask, "So, you promised to fuck me. Are you going to fuck me now?"

He crosses the room in two steps and demands, "Get on your hands and knees on the bed." His fingers are rough as they push hard in and out of my pussy. I feel the first wave of my orgasm and moan my appreciation.

I've gone to another world of pleasure, but he brings me back when I hear the foil package of the condom rip open and he warns me, "Here I come."

I chuckle at the double entendre. He enters me, and it takes a moment for me to adjust to his size. "God, you feel so good," I moan.

He pulls out slowly and then pushes in hard to the hilt until he hits my cervix. He speeds up, fucking me with rough intent, every thrust pushing me against the bed frame, marring my makeup, loosening my hair, abrading my nipples back and forth against the duvet.

He fucks me like I'm the enemy, like he can vanquish me. And maybe he can. He can invade my slick channel, forcing me to take him, giving friction and heat, pleasure and pain. I feel the rush of being spanked while he pulls my hair. The multiple sensations swirl even higher, tighter, sharper until I'm mindless on the end of his cock. I reach for my clit and circle it with frenzy.

"Make yourself come, baby," he growls between thrusts and spanks me again. His voice is harsh, roughened by sex, but determined.

His permission gives me the release I so urgently need. "Cameron," I moan as I see stars and my pussy clamps hard on his cock. My mind is drenched with need. It's hard to think. Hard to speak. It feels like I haven't spoken in a thousand years.

My mouth struggles to form words. "I want more."

"Do you like to be punished for being a bad girl?"

My heart beats faster. He turns me on with just the suggestion.

"Yes, please."

I NEED TO GET UP but I'm wrapped in his arms, Cameron's erection poking me in the back. Big, thick, and hard, it prods me for attention. I can't help myself as I disengage from his grasp and reach over to stroke his hard cock. It's positively huge. I could go down on him, but it doesn't give me a lot of satisfaction, and my sex is begging for his erection. Maybe if I climb on top of him and start riding him?

His breathing is rhythmic, and I believe he's still sound asleep. I remove a condom from where he stacked them on the bedside table, and he doesn't even flinch as I rip open the foil package with my teeth and roll it on his hard cock.

As I climb on and rock my hips to fill me with his steel rod, his eyes slowly flutter open and he gives me a lazy grin of pure pleasure. He reaches for my swollen tits bouncing just above his face and his mouth captures a nipple so he can bite it. The flicker of pain sends electrical jolts to my core, and I clench him hard.

He moans. "Oh, baby, fuck me."

My pussy is so full, and as I bounce faster and with each movement, he meets me with a hard pounding. With his hands on my hips, he pushes me deeper and deeper. A look of elation fills his face, and I hold on to his rock-hard pecs, impaling myself on him over and over.

Finally he moans and I collapse on top of him, out of breath, but he's too thorough a lover to let me go without my own orgasm. Rolling me onto my back, he slides his fingers inside me, stretching me wide, the slickness of my folds slurping as he brushes my G-spot while making sure to rub my clit. It's a different sensation, like he doesn't want me to finish; he alternates by pushing his cock deep inside each time my breath becomes labored and I get close to finishing, he stops and kisses my neck, the insides of my thighs, along my belly, or suckles my nipples. Once my breathing regulates, he starts all over. It's driving me crazy, but he keeps going, whispering, "I want to give you the best orgasm you've ever had."

His thick fingers are deep inside me, and his thumb strums my clit in a frenzy as he intermittently blows cool air on my hottest spot. Grasping the sheets, I swear I can see fireworks as my pussy explodes all over him and he leans in close, licking it up. "Mmm... you taste so sweet. I love it when you scream."

I think they heard my screams of passion in Arizona, Nevada, and Oregon. "Holy shit, that was mind-blowing," I say between breaths.

"That was a complete turn-on watching your face change each time you were close. I'm sure I'll think of that when I'm trying to work."

I can't imagine what that face must be, but I'm embarrassed nonetheless. No one would think he just had sex to look at him. Meanwhile, I'm rumpled and loose-limbed, every nerve of my body still tingling from aftershocks.

When he stares at me, it's as if every ounce of breath is taken from my lungs. Every time he kisses me I feel like the world stops, leaving the two of us to wander the Earth together. Every time he holds my face in his hands, it's like he's untying all of my knots.

He makes me feel so complete.

chapter
FOURTEEN

CAMERON

I GAZE AT HADLEE, her soft auburn curls draped across my pillow and a peaceful expression on her face. We've spent every night together this week, and I'm surprised by my comfort with it.

She is positively beautiful, both inside and out. Her emotions are not easily hidden on her innocent face, her pain evident in the crease of her lovely brow and the down curve of her full lips. But her eyes... her eyes show her soul. They're a deep pool of restless blue and gold, an ocean of hopeless optimism. As I stare into her eyes while we fuck, I know all the beauty of the universe could not even hope to compete with this simple thing: passion. It turns her eyes into orbs of the brightest fire, and in them, I read clearly that she would fight to the very last tear for her patients' welfare and for her friends. She won't let the world break her. Sure, she could cry, but she would never let me take her true self from her. She clings to it with passion. That passion makes her beautiful.

Her eyes open and she sees me watching her. I smile. "Hungry?"

She stretches like a cat. Her back arches as she extends her arms above her head, her magnificent nipple peeking from beneath the sheet. With a sigh, she seductively says, "I could use some food. Do you want to stay here or go out?"

I don't cook, but I don't want to go out either. "I rarely ate at home before you moved in. I don't have a lot here."

She sits up and untangles herself from the bedsheets. "I have eggs and can make omelets downstairs, if you're up for that?"

I'm shocked by her admission. I knew she grew up living next door to the Arnaults and most likely had cooks and lots of domestic help. "You cook?"

Staring at my tattoos, she licks her lips and my cock stirs. Having her for breakfast crosses my mind. She stares at my hardening cock. "I can make an omelet. I don't know if you'd call that cooking."

I kiss her on the top of her head, loving the way she smells. "We can make the omelets together." I want to spend the day with her. Hell, I want to spend the weekend with her. "Do you have plans today?"

She sits up and the sheets pool at her waist, exposing my favorite toys. "I was going to work on some things with my house, but you might be able to change my mind."

I want to spend time with her. I want to get to know everything about her. This is new for me. I struggle to be friends with the women I fuck. That isn't me right now. Usually I'm the guy who would rather chew his arm off than stay with a woman overnight, yet here I am thinking of spending the weekend with her. She may not be interested in my idea, but I can throw it out to her, and she can determine if it's a good one or not. "I thought we might take a ride out to Yosemite. If they have an opening at the Majestic Yosemite Hotel, we can stay there tonight. How does that sound?"

She thinks about it for a moment, and I'm not sure what I'll do if she refuses. I'm not ready for her to be apart from me. I want to spend more time with her, getting to know her and exploring more of her limits in bed.

She stares deep into my eyes, and I'm convinced she sees deep in my soul. "That sounds like a lot of fun." She jumps out of bed, talking to me as she walks naked along the hall. "Are you coming?"

Wait. What is she doing? "Where are you going?" I yell after her.

I hear the sliding glass door slide open. "I thought you wanted an omelet?"

I'm not completely surprised by her boldness. As I get to know her, little seems to scare her off. I scramble to grab my T-shirt and a pair of sweatpants. "Oh. Yes, I want breakfast. You've drained me of all my energy."

She smirks. "Well, I have a ton, so you must've pumped all your energy into me." She turns a beautiful shade of crimson and laughs a soft melody at her own joke.

"You're funny."

She smiles as she shrugs. "I try."

I realize that she's walking out and downstairs naked. My neighbors can be nosey; she'll freak out if they see her like this. "Wait, you're going downstairs naked?"

She turns to me with her brow knitted, clearly confused. "No one can see as I walk through the backyard, can they?"

I'm scrambling. "They might. But I have a key, so we can go

through the laundry room if you prefer."

She stops and turns around. "Why, Cameron, are you shy? Because I think your body is perfect in every way."

"As is yours, but I'm not willing to share it with my neighbors."

She keeps walking, and I'm left to follow her like the horny dog that I am.

She sneaks down the patio stairs and opens the door to her place, disappearing down the hall. I'm left standing at the bar in the kitchen. Gazing around the room, I see all the places I'd like to fuck her.

Bringing me back from my daydream, she emerges in a Clash T-shirt and gym shorts. "I have a T-shirt just like that."

"No you don't," she tells me with confidence.

I'm surprised by her certainty. How would she know if I had one or not? "Really I do."

She stares at me and repeats, "No, you don't. Because I stole this from you the night of Emerson and Dillon's wedding. You don't think I did the walk of shame in my bridesmaid dress, do you?"

I let out a deep belly laugh. Her confidence is such a turn-on. Finally, I admit, "I didn't even notice."

She steps in, circles her arms around my neck, and nibbles at my lower lip until I allow her entry and our tongues dance an aggressive tango in our mouths.

Breaking the kiss, she contends, "I hope it's because you were distracted by my absence in your bed."

"You have no idea."

"Good. Now could you shred this cheese?" she asks as she

hands me a nice block of cheddar and a grater. "I'll chop this pepper and some Canadian bacon and whip the eggs. Does that work for you?"

I love her post-sex confidence. "Absolutely."

We work in tandem for a while, and then she surprises me when she asks, "How do you think the 49ers are going to end up this year? They're having their typical tough start to the season, as always."

We've been hanging out for over a month and never spoken about sports. The last thing I expected was for her to ask me about the NFL. "You understand football?"

"Sort of. I still have my dad's season tickets. It was one way to spend time with him without a step-monster."

"Do you go to games?"

"If I can find someone to go with me, but I give most of them away. The seats are pretty decent. They're on the forty-five-yard line, and about twenty-five rows up. Far enough so you can see over the bench. I wish the team were better. Is there any hope in my lifetime, or should I give up the tickets?"

I'm stunned. "Don't give up those tickets. They're getting better. I'm happy to go with you to some of the games this fall. I can't believe you like football."

"I like baseball, too. I'm a big Giants fan."

She is beautiful, amazing in bed, and loves sports. How could I get any luckier? "You are a guy's wet dream. You do get that, right?"

Dripping with sarcasm, she tells me, "Sure. That's why I've had two serious boyfriends in my entire life."

I'm taken aback by her admission. "Trust me when I tell you, not only are you beautiful, but you like sports, which makes you a rock star in my book."

Shyly, she admits, "Well, right now that's the only book I care about."

She plates the omelets, and we sit at the table. I take a bite, and I'm convinced this is the best omelet I've ever had. "This is amazing. There's a bit of a kick. What's different?"

"I added some shakes of Tabasco sauce while you were making the Nespressos."

What can't this girl do? "You're an incredible cook."

"I had a great helper." Changing subjects, she asks, "What should I wear to ride on the Harley?"

As much as I'd love to have her wrapped around me for a three-hour drive out to Yosemite, it isn't practical without good protection. "How about we go in my car? It's a bit more comfortable than the motorcycle, and we can shop for leathers for you before we go for a long ride on the Harley."

"Leathers?"

"We want to cover those fine legs and arms with good leather chaps and a jacket. Plus, we should get you your own helmet."

"Makes sense." She places her finger seductively in her mouth. "And here I was hoping you wanted me fit with a leather corset and thong."

I stop mid-bite. "Do you understand how hot that makes me?"

She giggles. "I'm up for whatever floats your boat except for minors, and I'm not too keen on adding other people into the mix. But I love the spanking. I've never done that before. When you threatened to tie me up, I think I had an actual orgasm at the thought."

"Fuck, girl. You are my wet dream."

"Good, because you're my wet dream. Just enough bad boy to get me all excited."

I guess this is as good a time as any to find out if she's into what I like. "I'm not sure I'll be able to wait until we get to the Majestic to fuck you tonight."

"Well, I suppose you'll have to pack a blanket for some roadside fucking."

Did she just tell me she's willing to have sex in public? I'm practically speechless as she lifts her shirt, exposing her exquisite breasts, the nipples begging to be touched and played with. My mouth drops open as she twists and pulls on them before bringing her breast to her mouth and licking the tip. "Mmm...."

"Fuck. That's it. Get your ass to your room and assume the position."

"What's the position?" she asks innocently.

"I want you naked, on your hands and knees on your bed," I growl.

She grins widely and scampers off, obviously excited. She's as horny as I am.

I eat the last few bites of my breakfast; I'm going to need my energy. Before I go find her, I run upstairs to grab a few condoms and a sex toy.

When I stop at the threshold to her room, I'm greeted by the most glorious sight. She's on her hands and knees, her pink slit glistening as it faces me. I stare at her reflection in the mirror—her eyes are closed and she's playing with herself, her fingers swirling around her clit as she rocks back and forth. My cock hurts from straining against the zipper in my jeans. I undress as I watch the show she's giving me, and it's almost painful to remove my boxers over my steel rod. The wet sounds and her labored breathing mean she's close. I want to hear her call my name as I make her come.

chapter
FIFTEEN

HADLEE

I DON'T UNDERSTAND why I'm so open with Cameron. I've had two long-term partners with long periods of celibacy in between. I'm a sexual person, and I masturbate often. I have toys, and I've always been curious about kinky sex. With Cameron, when he spanks me, it gets my motor running. Knowing Cameron is a bad boy underneath his cool exterior excites me. Maybe that's why I can be myself. I'm not uncomfortable with him in the least. I feel safe with him. He doesn't point out the dimples in my thighs, the pudge around my middle, my overly large breasts—believe it or not, most men don't really like more than a handful—or seem to mind my red hair.

I quickly undress and crawl onto my bed, so the first view he'll have is of my wet slit. I watch myself in the mirrored closet doors, and I'm so excited I begin playing with my slick channel. Circling my clit, I have a small orgasm, and our eyes meet as he watches me play with myself.

I lick my fingers. "Did you enjoy the show?"

I stare at his raging erection as he strokes himself. "I would say so. But I think you'll need to be punished for taking away my enjoyment from giving you pleasure."

I wiggle my ass in the air. "I've been naughty. I think you'll have to punish me."

He brings something from behind his back and asks, "Have you ever seen these before?"

I shake my head and whisper, "No."

He squeezes the pincher and they open and close, but they don't seem to close completely. "These are adjustable nipple clamps. You enjoy nipple play, and I was wondering if you'd be willing to try them."

I can't take my eyes off the clamp as I nod, my body involuntarily quivering from a small orgasm.

As he approaches, I notice they're jeweled. He tells me, "These screws here will keep the clamp from pinching too tight. We want them to add good pressure and some pain, but not too much."

He glances at me expectantly. I bite my lower lip and nod, and he demands, "Turn around."

I kneel on the bed facing him. He caresses my breast roughly and brings the nipple to his mouth, thoroughly licking and sucking it to a hard nub. He pulls it taut and attaches the first clamp with a tight pinch that sends jolts to my core as I moan my appreciation. He then does the same to my other nipple. I'm becoming desperate for friction against my clit, but each time I move my hand to my pussy, he pushes it away. Once both nipples are secured in the clamps, he pulls on the chain connecting them and I moan in ecstasy again.

"I love how responsive you are," he whispers. "Lie on your back and open your legs."

He dives in and eats my pussy as if he hasn't had a meal in

days. His fingers push deep inside as he finds that spot, and I'm so aroused. Lathering my clit with his mouth, he sucks and strums it until I'm close to reaching my pinnacle. Then he stops.

What? Don't stop! I'm almost there.

"Naughty girls don't get to come that easily."

I can't help but be a little disappointed.

"Roll over and show me that ivory ass of yours."

I do as he asks and wave my ass in the air at him. The chains shift, and the combination of the clamps with the weight of my breasts and the friction of the quilt below me almost have me overwhelmed by my arousal. "Please, Cameron," I beg.

"You want to come?" he snarls.

"Yes, please." My hips move voluntarily as I search for anything to bring me relief. He caresses my ass and then spanks me hard. I moan just as he slams his cock inside. He slaps my backside again, and I clamp down on him inside of me.

He pounds me hard and fast, my every nerve on fire as his long fingers adeptly circle my clit.

I can't hold back any longer.

"Hadlee, come for me."

He grunts his orgasm while I moan his name.

Collapsing next to me on the bed, he removes the nipple clamps, and the pain and pleasure make me almost delirious.

"Well, what do you think of the clamps?"

"Holy shit, that was a totally new sensation. That was fucking unbelievable."

"Shit! I forgot to wear a condom. I swear I don't have any STDs. You have an IUD, right? I was surprised by you masturbating when I came in, and I just dove right in."

Giggling, I tell him, "Yes, you sure did dive in. I've never been super comfortable receiving oral sex, but you are mind-blowing. And yes, I have an IUD."

"If you keep going like this, we won't make it to Yosemite," he warns.

I guess it's time to come back to reality. "I suppose we should do something other than fuck."

His eyes are smoldering, clearly struggling with the idea of going out or staying in all weekend.

"Have you ever had a blow job while driving?" I ask with as much innocence as a girl who just got fucked hard while wearing nipple clamps and getting spanked possibly could.

"No, and I'd be afraid I'd crash my Porsche."

"Okay fine, I won't do that, but you have to promise me you'll let me finish you off with just my mouth at some point this weekend."

"Trust me, you won't have to beg. I just believe your orgasms are more important to me than my own."

chapter
SIXTEEN

CAMERON

I DRIVE A SLATE GRAY PORSCHE 918 SPYDER that most women would swoon over. It appeals to the environmentalist as a hybrid electric car, but the cockpit looks like it belongs in a video game. For a million-dollar vehicle, it's a gearhead's dream, and I love it. We cruise along the freeway, traveling east across the desert valley to one of America's most stunning locations. Hadlee is sitting in the front passenger seat with so much soft leather around her, and the engine is so quiet I can hear her breathe. At eighty miles per hour, the engine is only idling in electric mode. But I can feel the power. Four thousand pounds of German engineering. With only nine hundred and eighteen made each year, this car turns heads.

Hadlee reaches over and holds my hand. Not since my mother died have I had someone show me this much affection, and I like it. As we pass through the wind turbine farms, the miles of almond trees, it's open road most of the time.

I turn the music up and show her what a terrible singer I am as Robert Palmer's "Addicted to Love" plays and we both sing along. She has a tremendous voice. I lower the volume so I can hear her, and she blushes. "Turn the music back up. My voice is like fingernails on a chalkboard."

"No, you're really a great singer."

"I think you're in an after-sex delusion."

"Is that a real thing?"

With complete seriousness, she says, "Oh, absolutely. They've done tons of studies, and I've read them. I'm a doctor, you know." It isn't until she's done that I realize she's being facetious.

She is truly funny, and I laugh loud and hard. "You almost had me with that."

"There is no way you're that gullible."

"When you put it that way, of course not." To get myself out of trouble, I ask, "If you were in a band, what type of music would you sing, and what would you name your band?"

"That's a good question. Let's see... I'm not good enough to headline a band, so calling it 'Hadlee Ford' would be a real loser. I would sing fun and upbeat pop and call us the...." She's actually thinking about this, and we drive a couple minutes in silence before she continues. "We'd call ourselves 'The Wayward Children.'"

"'The Wayward Children'? Where did that come from?"

"I thought 'The Naughty Doctors' sounded like a porn title, so I went with a different word for disobedient. And since I'm a pediatrician and love children, I ended it with that."

"That's some interesting logic, but the band title does work with your genre."

"What about you?"

"I know given the tattoos you'd think I'd want to be in a heavy metal band or maybe alternative, but I think if I could sing, I would be like Michael Bublé. I'm nowhere near as creative as you are though, so we would call ourselves 'Cameron and the Band.'"

I change my iPod to play Michael Bublé over the stereo, and I belt out "All I Do is Dream of You."

She puts her hand on my arm and says with great sincerity, "Please keep your day job."

"Hey! Was I that bad?"

She's laughing so hard she wipes a tear from her eye. "No, not at all."

We ride in comfortable silence as we sing to the California desert valley and ranches.

We start to approach Yosemite, driving uphill through the town of Midpines. The landscape changes and the temperature drops slightly as the road parallels the Merced River. I stare out at the redbud trees along its banks sprouting magenta-colored flowers, the river rising high enough to accommodate white-water rafters.

"Have you ever been whitewater rafting?" I ask.

"I did as a girl when I went to summer camp, but I'm not a great swimmer. I can swim, but the whitewater's a little intimidating. How about you?"

"Dillon, Mason, and I went once. Dillon got knocked from the boat, and he sank, right to the bottom and scared the guide. He was fine but seemed like a drowned rat when he finally figured out that if he stood up, the water was at his waist. We all laugh about it when it comes up."

As we pull up to the entrance gate at Yosemite National Park, the attendant greets us. "Welcome to Yosemite. Heading up to the Majestic Yosemite Hotel?"

I hand him my national park pass. "Yes, we are."

"Do you need a map?"

I start to tell him, "No," because I come here often to ride my motorcycle, but Hadlee most likely doesn't know the park as well as I do. "Yes, please."

He hands me my season pass along with the map, and I pass it all to Hadlee. We follow the signs marked Bridalveil Fall, stopping in the parking lot just before we reach the tunnel. It offers a stunning panoramic view of the Yosemite Valley, where we can see all its icons in one vista: El Capitan, Bridalveil Fall, and Half Dome. We take a selfie with the stunning background.

"This is my favorite spot," I tell Hadlee.

"I can see why. Mother Nature is staggering in her beauty."

Returning to the car, we head off to the Majestic Yosemite Hotel. For decades the Majestic was called the Ahwahnee Hotel, but the new owners changed the name a few years ago. It's the finest hotel in the National Park system.

As we pull up to the front of the hotel, Hadlee gushes, "It's magnificent."

"It was built in the 1920s, the location carefully chosen due to its exposure to Yosemite's most famous residents"—I point to each in turn—"Glacier Point, Yosemite Falls, and Half Dome."

"How often do you come here on your bike?"

"My club does two trips a year, and I might do two more depending on how work is going."

"You have a very stressful job."

"I do, but yours is probably more stressful."

"Diagnosing ear infections or the flu, and helping parents cope with things like ADHD or asthma isn't necessarily stressful."

"Those things aren't, but you just had to tell a family their daughter has cancer. That had to wreck you."

"It did and does, but thankfully I only do that a few times a year."

When I hand the keys to the valet, Hadlee leans over and asks, "Are you nervous?"

"Nah, it's only a car. After losing my mom the way I did, I recognize that cars are replaceable."

"You do understand they're going to pull a *Ferris Bueller* and take it for a joyride."

I hold up the fob. "They can only go about a half of a mile before the engine dies since they only have the valet key."

We walk into the hotel hand in hand, a "Wow!" escaping her as she takes in the lobby.

The design of the Majestic is a mix of Native American, Middle Eastern, Art Deco, and the Arts and Crafts movement. "The hotel's wood-like façade is actually made of concrete to protect the historic building from fires, which have taken other park hotels," I tell her.

She reaches into her bag, trying to get her wallet out among all the other contents.

"What are you thinking?" I ask.

"Getting my wallet. I'm not completely broke. You drove, so I can get the room."

"Are you crazy? Don't worry. I got this. In fact, let me be clear—I don't want your wallet to make an appearance all weekend. This entire trip is my treat. Now head over there to the Great Lounge and check out the floor-to-ceiling windows and stunning views."

If she thinks she can change my mind, she's nuts. She has

enough bills to worry about, and I can easily afford this. Plus there's something in me that wants to treat her like the princess I think she is.

I go to the front desk and learn they've had a cancellation for one of the free-standing cottages on the hotel grounds. *Awesome!*

After checking in, I go in search of her. She's facing the window, and I put my arms around her and kiss her neck.

"Isn't this beautiful?" she murmurs.

I smell her perfume and am so distracted by her beauty that all I can do is agree.

We follow the bellman with our overnight bags to our cottage, which is tucked away amongst the dogwoods and pine trees. He tells us, "With the renovation by the new owners, the cottages have most modern amenities, including TV, phone, and a small fridge, but there's no A/C. The ceiling fan surprisingly makes up for it in the heat, and you can open your windows, but make sure you don't leave any food out."

"Why?" Hadlee asks.

"The bears will come. They can't get in, but they can do damage."

She gives me a terrified look. I put my arm around her and give her an assuring hug. "Don't worry, I'll protect you."

He gives us a quick tour of the room, and I tip him before he leaves. Turning to her, I lean in and give her a soft, gentle kiss. The cottage has a large four-poster bed that faces the woods, and I want to take her in it. "You know, I have thoughts of you tied up spread-eagle on this bed and all the naughty things I want to do to you."

In a lusty, sexy voice, she says, "While incredibly tempting, we need to get out and explore some of the park."

I press my erection into her back. "So true, but we still have tonight."

She turns around to face me and puts her arms around my neck. "That's what I'm counting on." She runs her finger down the middle of my chest and stops below the pelvic bone. My cock is so hard right now, I'm sure I'm going to get blue-balls.

We walk to the lobby to catch the shuttle for a two-hour tour. As we wait, several of the guys are talking about my car, which is parked front and center.

"Man, can you imagine that thing?"

"Dude, that car can go 300 miles an hour on a good straight-away."

"The McLaren P1 is better."

Hadlee raises her eyebrows at me, and I shrug. "Mason thinks that, too."

The guys turn to me and asks, "What do you think?"

I cross my arms and say, "It is a pretty ostentatious car."

"No kidding. Who spends a million dollars on a car like that? I mean, what a waste of a million."

The shuttle arrives and we pile in, Hadlee snuggling up close to me. "You're very bad. You had those guys eating out of your hand. If you'd admitted it was your car, they would've abandoned the tours and begged to drive it."

"Why do you think I didn't volunteer that information? I don't disagree with anything they said, but I love my car. I rarely drive it because it isn't fun in the city with all the traffic and lights."

The two-hour guided tour takes us from location to location, and the park ranger gives wonderful descriptions of the valley's famous landmarks and history.

When we return to the Majestic, we walk hand in hand to the cottage. We have two hours before our dinner reservation. I wouldn't mind some afternoon delight, but when we enter, Hadlee kisses me. "You realize there's this god who's been keeping me up all night, right? Do you mind if I take a nap before we go to dinner?"

My disappointment must be obvious, as she bites at my lower lip and reaches for my cock. "I want all the energy I can get for tonight."

"I expect a late night, so maybe we both should take a nap."

I'm stunned when Hadlee strips to her thong and climbs under the covers. I join her in my boxers and spoon her. The next thing I know, the alarm on my phone is going off.

I don't think I've ever slept that soundly with a woman before. She stretches into me, then reaches for my hard cock and strokes it. "Maybe we should order room service."

"You read my mind, but I want to show you the Ahwahnee Dining Room. It has large picture windows overlooking the valley where we can watch the sunset."

She bends over me, pulls my dick through the hole in the front of my boxers, and takes it deep in her mouth. Her ass close to my shoulder, I move her thong aside and explore her slick channel, probing in and out with one finger before adding another. She moans, and the vibrations on my cock have me rethinking my evening plans.

Suddenly she stops and turns to me. "I needed a taste before dinner."

"Fuck, woman. I'm going to go to dinner with a raging hard-on."

"Good. It gives you something to look forward to."

chapter SEVENTEEN

HADLEE

I CAN'T SEEM TO GET ENOUGH OF HIM. He matches my sex drive incredibly well. I swear the man gives new meaning to multiple orgasms. And Jesus, that tongue. Holy cow.

As I think about it, he's not only a sex machine, he's so much more. He's kindhearted, funny as can be, and generous to a fault, both with his time to his clients, friends, and to me as well as financially. He still hasn't cashed any of the checks I've left for him for rent, and he won't let me pay anything toward this weekend—such a gentleman.

I'm falling for him, and falling hard.

I've never been confident enough to walk around naked, but I do with him. He's seen me at my most vulnerable, but he seems to like my imperfections. As an old boyfriend pointed out to me, "A guy doesn't care what you look like as long as you're naked," so I try to muster the confidence to have my tits out and pointing to the ground. Nothing sexy there, I think, but Cameron always stares, his eyes hooded in pure lust.

I shower, and the humidity gives my auburn curls the perfect amount of bounce. We work in tandem in the cramped bathroom like a well-choreographed dance. He hums a tune I can't quite make out.

"What is that song?"

He quirks his lips. "You need to figure it out."

I throw a towel at him. "Oh, just you wait."

His dazzling smile melts my heart.

Dressing in the light green sundress Jennifer picked out, which makes my waist appear small and my tits a little less distracting—if that's even possible—I add a pair of skintone stiletto sandal. Cameron has a good six inches on me, but these shoes bring me closer in height.

I walk out of the bathroom, and while putting in my mother's pearl earrings, I turn to him and ask, "Can you please zip my dress?"

He uses the opportunity to reach in and play with my breasts, teasing me. Heat rushes to my groin. "Cameron, I thought you wanted to eat in the dining room?" I moan.

"Okay. I'll give you a break before I tie you to the bed after dinner and we see how many orgasms you can have tonight."

I stand on my tiptoes and kiss him deeply. "Keep talking like that and we won't make it out of here."

As we walk out of the cottage and over to the main dining room, I glance at Cameron. He's wearing khaki pants and a nice light blue collared shirt with a pair of Gucci loafers. With his slicked-back hair, he almost seems like a different person. Not one piece of ink is showing. He's like a conservative banker dressed for a casual dinner, but underneath I know he's all bad boy. I love that this is what most people see, and I'm one of the few who knows what hides beneath.

"You're very handsome tonight, but I can't wait to peel you out of those clothes and play with your dragon. By the way, I may have forgotten to wear panties tonight."

I could swear his pants tent a little. "You are very naughty," he growls.

"And you love it."

He gives my breast a playful tweak, and I moan involuntarily.

We arrive at the hostess stand, and Cameron gives her his name. "My apologies, but your table isn't quite ready yet," she tells us. "If you like live music, you can enjoy the evening's piano player at Ahwahnee Bar and enjoy a drink on the house."

We take our place in the bar, Cameron orders two glasses of scotch, and we enjoy listening to the piano player as he goes through several jazz and contemporary songs. When the hostess finds us, Cameron stands and places a twenty-dollar bill in tip jar, and the pianist thanks him as we walk to our table.

The dining room is long and narrow with a stepped design, giving each table a private booth feeling. There isn't a bad seat in the room as it overlooks the big picture window. We take our seats, sitting so close our knees touch, and he runs his hand along my leg, getting closer and closer to my core as we look over the menu. It features California cuisine with local ingredients that are organic and sustainably harvested.

"Do you have a preference for wine?" Cameron asks.

"I drink it all—even out of a box."

"They have my favorite, Stags Leap, but it's only by the bottle. Hmm. That's a lot of wine for what we talked about doing tonight."

"What do you mean?"

He leans in and says so only I can hear, "I won't tie you up unless you are 100 percent sober."

"That makes sense. I've already had a glass of scotch though, so technically I'm not 100 percent sober for six to eight hours."

He appears crestfallen. "I'll order the wine, but do understand that I'm looking forward to tying you up and enjoying giving you hours and hours of pleasure."

Just the thought of all the pleasure he's promising makes me shudder with excitement. "I hope it doesn't mean we still can't enjoy a fun night after dinner," I reply.

He trails his finger up my thigh. I open my legs to allow him entrance, and he rubs at my center. "I would hope not."

I'm grateful the tablecloth is long and no one can see his hands explore. We'll have sex here at the table if I don't change the subject. "Even at night, this is beautiful. What's the most beautiful place you've ever been?"

His finger continues to work its ministrations. "Well, I didn't grow up with much money, so I've only traveled over the last few years. I love it here at Yosemite, and I loved Yellowstone earlier this year, though I don't know if I can choose between the two. What about you?"

"San Francisco is probably my favorite. I love the beach by the Marina where you can watch the sun set behind the Golden Gate Bridge."

"That's definitely a top ten. I need to write a bucket list. I think about it, but I haven't done it yet."

"A bucket list for sex?" I ask innocently.

"We can do that together, too." Leaning in, he kisses me, and then we hear our waiter clear his throat.

"Good evening. My name is Phillip, and helping me tonight are Grace and Jack. May I start you with a drink?"

Cameron orders the Stags Leap wine, and Phillip shares the specials. I've decided on what I want for dinner. When he returns with the wine, he offers Cameron a sample, which he swirls in his glass before tasting it. He nods. "That's perfect."

A glass is poured for me and then for Cameron, and I order the swordfish while Cameron goes for the buffalo.

While we wait for our meal, we drink and we talk. "You're a successful doctor in San Francisco with a group of friends who are closer than most families. Are there things you first saw as failures that turned out good in your life, and now you're proud of?" Cameron asks me.

"That's a great question." I think about it a moment. "I guess the biggest failure was when my dad died when I was a sophomore in college, and I learned the trust fund I'd come to count on had been spent by my stepmother. She spent all my dad's money on things she could give to her kids."

"You've said that before, but what does that mean, 'things she could give her kids'?"

"My father was ill, and she bought all sorts of property—commercial and private—in her own name. Upon her death, it'll go to her children, and she was very clear that it wouldn't be coming to me because she was giving me $200,000 instead."

"What did the lawyer say?"

"He was angry because of everything she did, but it was allowed under the terms of my father's estate. He was alive but not coherent when she did it."

"That's awful."

"I know that doesn't sound like much of a failure, but it was scary. I've never known debt, and my dad had always taught me financial responsibility, but I always figured I'd be able to practice medicine to underserved communities and not have to worry about a paycheck, and that changed."

Our dinner arrives, and after we toast to being in such a beautiful venue, I continue. "But I learned a lot about myself and my friends. I never cared about money. Granted, I was disappointed that I needed a paycheck so I had a roof over my head and food on the table, but I still work with an underserved community, and my friends are amazing. I may not always be able to join them on expensive shopping trips, but I wear jeans and a lab coat all day. Getting vomit or poop on nice clothes isn't practical. And as for fancy vacations, sometimes I go, and sometimes they go without me, which is fine, too."

"You get vomited and pooped on often?"

I laugh. "Virtually every day. It doesn't bother me though. It comes with the job."

"You're astounding."

I know I'm blushing a brilliant shade of red. "What about you?"

He stares at me for a beat before responding. "Dillon and Mason know, but don't tell anyone this, I got fired from my first job out of Stanford."

"You were fired?"

"I was. I worked for a large company, and I disagreed with my manager on how the software should be designed. He was much smarter than I was, and I was an ass. I totally deserved it. But I was only unemployed for half a day, thanks to Dillon, before I joined a start-up. I loved the freedom that came with working for a small company. I learned all sorts of roles and got to try out different jobs, which has really helped me understand why small companies behave the way they do. Plus, the company I went to is where I made my first million."

"Maybe when you decide to tattoo your legs, you can do a phoenix."

He laughs. "That would work. Actually, I'm done. The dragon has a meaning to me. It symbolizes the disease that took my mother away from me. I was angry for a long time, but with encouragement from Dillon and Mason, I sat with a therapist and worked through most of it. I'm still upset with my dad, because of what happened to my mother, but at some point, it'll kill me if I can't get beyond it."

"Letting go is incredibly powerful."

"You did the same thing."

"I guess I did."

We enjoy the rest of our dinner and finish the bottle of wine. My mind floats, and I now understand why he wants me fully aware of myself to be tied up. The idea of submitting to him excites me, but we'll wait for now. We have time.

Once he pays for dinner, we walk to our cottage holding hands, stopping to listen to the waterfall. His face is lit by the moon, and I step in and kiss him. It starts tentatively but quickly becomes aggressive.

Grinding his erection into my stomach, he growls, "I want you."

I rest a hand at his waist and ask, "Does outside work for you?"

"Woman, you are going to kill me."

"Is that a yes or a no?" I ask as I get on my knees and begin to unbutton his pants when we hear a woman laugh. She's close.

Eyes wide, Cameron helps me stand. "Let's take this inside."

We walk quickly to our cottage, and the door is hardly closed when we continue where we left off, though he won't let me finish him. "I have other plans for you," he tells me before bending me over the back of the couch with only the moon cascading into the living area. He lifts the skirt of my dress and takes me in one swift move.

chapter EIGHTEEN

CAMERON

SITTING AT MY DESK, I'm distracted by a gray, cloudy, and foggy San Francisco morning. Hadlee and my trip to Yosemite were surprisingly fun. We spent time driving and exploring during the day, and at night she enjoyed whatever I was into and asked for more.

A weekend is almost a whole new thing for me. Maybe it is because she lives downstairs? I don't know why I have this level of comfort with Hadlee, but I love spending time with her. And it just isn't the sex—though that's positively incredible. It's so much more.

God, her lips, the look on her face when she's riding me, her passion for her patients and how she lights up when she talks about them. Plus her tits are perfect, and she even let me fuck them this weekend.

I remember her jasmine smell and the perfect wake-up call I got this morning. After going down on me to make sure I was wet and lubricated, she climbed on top of me and turned around, leaving me with the most fantastic view of her ass. It's flawless, and I love the bit of jiggle as she bounced on my cock. I couldn't help but reach out and caress her before I slapped it to give it a nice pink handprint. I was thinking how I really wanted to fuck her ass, but then she distracted me by squeezing my balls as she rode me. I didn't want it to end, and I experienced the strongest, loudest orgasm I've ever had. The memory of working my cock in and out of her wet, tight slit while she played with my balls excites me all over again.

I've heard my buddies talk about the whole package, and I never understood it, but I'm beginning to think Hadlee is the whole package for me.

Goddamn, I love the sex with her. I can't get enough of her. My cock is rock-hard whenever she's not around, thinking about the bright red handprints I'm leaving all over her beautiful heart-shaped ass. Smiling to myself, I wonder if she'll be able to sit today.

I'm still lost in my fantasies when my admin sticks her head in. "Um, Cameron? Your dad is in reception. Were you expecting him?"

Shit. Crap. Fuck. "Nope. I'll go see what he needs." I leave my office and head toward the reception area.

As I approach, I'm sure I can smell him—stale cigarettes and booze leaking from his pores. I could've cared less if I ever laid eyes on him again and yet he's like a bad penny that always turns up. In a strained voice, I ask, "What's up, Dad?"

"Hey... Cam," he slurs. "I was in the neighborhood and thought I'd check out your new digs."

I stand, spreading my arms to showcase the open-floor plan of our offices. "Here it is. Let's walk downstairs to Starbucks and pick you up a strong cup of black coffee."

My dad is an alcoholic. Years of alcohol abuse has left his cheeks rosy and his mind dull-witted. He knows drying out would be a painful process, and he's never had the intention of going through it. He's determined to stay drunk until he dies.

"Sure. Great. I have some things to tell you."

I lead him to the elevator. After we step in and the doors shut, I turn to him. "Why are you here? Do you need money?"

"No! I had an appointment in the city, and I thought I would stop by. I haven't seen you in a while."

"Where's Jean?" Jean is my dad's girlfriend and fellow drunk buddy. They've been together for close to a decade, though I don't understand why she stays with him beyond that he's someone to drink with.

"She left me last year."

I'm taken aback by this. He never told me. Not that I'd care, of course. "No real surprise."

"I'm not drunk. I'm loopy from a few tests they gave me this morning is all." He does seem more lucid than he is when he's drunk. Maybe he's actually telling me the truth.

We get our coffees and sit. Staring deep into his drink, he starts. "Listen, Cam...." *Ah, here it is.* "I have to return for a follow-up appointment tomorrow by seven. Can I crash at your place tonight? I won't get in the way. I can sleep on the couch or even the floor if you don't have any room for me."

I don't want him to stay, but he seems rather pathetic, and I'm not completely heartless. "Yeah. Sure. I have a guest room you can stay in."

I don't think I've seen my dad in almost five years. When I was growing up, so much damage was done when he was drunk and would yell at me. Every mean thing he'd thought but knew better than to say when he was sober came flooding out. When he saw the hurt in his opponent's eyes, he never backed off, only dug deeper, like a hunter at the first sign of blood. So when I got a full-ride scholarship to Stanford at eighteen, I never went home unless I absolutely had to.

The conversation stalls. We seem more like strangers than we do father and son. Finally, he looks up and asks, “You got a cute girl?”

That’s rich coming from him. He was no role model when it came to women. I can’t remember when he didn’t have a beer in his hands. He was in the car the night my mom died. She was sober and driving him home when they were hit by a drunk driver. She was killed on impact. He lived, and I’ve wished every day that he was the one who’d died and not my mom. It’s all his fault. He may not have been driving, but had he been sober, he could’ve driven himself home. I was twelve, and we became strangers living under the same roof.

“You know me. I’m not very good with girls.”

“You were always a chick magnet in school. Just like your old man.”

“Well, once they realize how fucked up I am, they move on.”

He picks at the seam of his paper cup. “That’s probably my fault.”

“You won’t get any arguments from me.” There’s obvious pain in his eyes at my jab, but frankly I don’t care.

Reaching into my pocket, I pull out my house key and slide it across the table. “Here’s my key. The alarm code is mom’s birthday.” I write my home address and my mom’s birthday on the back of my business card and hand it to him. "The guest room is the first room on the right."

"Thanks, Cam." Looking it over, he asks, "What time will you be home?"

I'm tired, and I wanted to go home early, but now I'm reconsidering. There're days that the exhaustion is both physical and mental. My body needs to rest, yet my mind needs it to move, to burn the anxiety right out. I may still leave early, but maybe I'll hit the gym. I work out to take the edge off and have control. I once thought my old man weak for depending on alcohol like he does, and I'm determined to keep control of my intake. I won't be the same way. "It'll be late."

He nods and says, "Well, thanks for allowing me to stay."

As we walk out, he heads toward the bus stop. I ask, "You want money for a cab?"

With a deep pull on a cigarette, he shakes his head. "Nah. I don't have much to do when I get there, so it's okay if it takes a while to get to your place."

I tell him what buses to take and hand him a twenty-dollar bill. "I'm not sure if there's much in the fridge, so you may want to grab something on the way. There's a decent burger place right at the bus stop by my house."

He stares at the bill cautiously before he takes it. "Sure. Thanks."

I head to my office deep in thought about my childhood before and after my mom died. It was like she took all the sunlight with her when she was killed. His visit has ruined my afternoon.

Emerson stops me in the kitchen as I'm scrounging for a late lunch. "I hear your dad's in town. Are we all going to get to meet him?"

"Probably not. He's just here for some meetings."

Dillon was my college roommate, and he only met my dad once at graduation. I don't talk about my family at all, and I prefer to keep it that way, but I have a feeling I won't get away with that right now.

"Oh, that's cool. You never talk about him. What does he do?"

There's no value in lying or glorifying him in any way. "He's a sheet metal worker when he's sober."

She looks shocked. "Ahh. Well, we'd love to meet him if you're up for that."

"Thanks, but I think he's heading home tomorrow." I've found an apple, cashews, a yogurt, and some peanut butter crackers. I grab a Diet Coke and head to my office. Not the best lunch, but it's filling enough to hold me over.

Sitting behind my desk once again, my mind drifts to my dad. Something's off, but I'm not sure I actually care.

chapter NINETEEN

HADLEE

DETERMINATION DRIVES ME ON. I'm still reeling from Lilly's sad news. It reminds me that life isn't fair. No child should ever get cancer, pure and simple.

I wipe my face clean as if a screen had been pulled down to hide my emotions and hurry along, ready for a glass of wine and relaxation. It's beginning to get dark, the coming night teasing the sky into twilight. Fear sits heavy on my heart as I walk as fast as I can. I saw her sister today, and her mother is an understandable wreck. Eyes plastered to the floor, she didn't say much, just stared at her shoes. I know she's trying to be strong for her other kids, and it breaks my heart.

It's a crap day. I could use a drink, but I don't want to go out with the girls. I'm hoping Cameron will help me take my mind off it all. My ass is nicely tender and each time I sit, I'm reminded of him and his beautiful cock and what it does to me. It's a good thing I don't have to sit too often at work.

I open the door to my apartment, and though it's later than I had wanted to be home, the bottle of shiraz is calling my name. I change into a black pair of yoga pants and a UCSF Medical School sweatshirt. Walking into the kitchen to grab my wine, I see a man sitting outside on the patio. There isn't any way to get to the patio without going through my place or Cameron's, so I figure he must know Cameron.

With the bottle and two glasses, I slide open the door. "Hi. I'm Hadlee."

He stands. "Hi, I'm Michael, Cameron's father."

I can see the resemblance. They're both similar in height at over six feet tall. Michael's hair is mostly gray, but when he smiles, I can see the shared physical characteristics. "So nice to meet you. I have a bottle of wine. Would you like a glass?"

He holds up a glass with a clear liquid and explains, "I already have a glass, but thank you."

I can't help but be disappointed that Cameron has company. I don't want to interrupt, so I ask tentatively, "Do you mind if I join you?"

I notice his eyes are glazed and have a slight hue of yellow, and he's dressed in clean but well-worn clothes. He tilts his head to the side. "You live with Cameron?"

"Oh, no. I'm his tenant and... friend." After an awkward pause, I share, "My house was destroyed by a fire a few months ago, and Cameron was between tenants, so he's renting it to me."

He stumbles as he attempts to get up to leave. "Sorry, that must mean this is your backyard. I'll get out of your way."

I reach for his arm and softly say, "No. Please stay. Cameron and I have been friends for a while, but we're part of a larger group. Tell me about him."

He sits and a broad smile crosses his face. He's nostalgic. "He was always so smart."

I nod. "I believe that."

"You two aren't dating?"

Well, technically we aren't dating, we're only fucking. "No, we're not dating. What brings you to San Francisco?"

"I have an appointment in the morning."

I can tell he's sick. My medical school training tells me the yellow tone of his skin means it's most likely cirrhosis of the liver or possibly liver cancer. If I had to guess, it's a terminal diagnosis unless he can get on the transplant list. "Good luck with your appointment."

We sit in silence, listening to the city as the white noise of the traffic permeates the air.

Out of nowhere, Michael shares, "I was a bad parent, though I never meant to be." Nodding, he rambles, "I wonder if it's what happens when you take a love that strong and mix it with fear and alcohol. Like every decision ever made, they're based on a combination of what I was sure was true and my love for Cam's mother—a core motivation, I guess. She was my whole world. After she died, alcohol and love came together to make a pushiness to drive my son forward, while at the same time addressing the fear that I didn't want him to be like me—in a crap job barely able to make ends meet."

"We all do the best we can," I sympathize.

Sitting quietly for a moment, he mumbles, "My love was never conditional or with an expiration date with him, but in my failure to just tell him that I loved him, I failed him in the worst possible way. All my son ever needed to know was that I'd love him no matter what he chose to do with his life, and that he was free to make his own choices."

I pat his hand in hopes of reassuring him. It's very normal to rethink your mistakes when faced with a terminal illness. I don't understand their history, and beyond encouraging him to tell Cameron all of this, there isn't much I can do.

It's just after 11:30 p.m. when Cameron comes home, opening his back door and peering down at us. "I see you two met. Sorry I didn't call you to tell you he'd be here."

We don't have that kind of relationship where we check in with each other, so I'm not upset that he didn't call, but he doesn't seem too thrilled that his dad's here and talking to me. I want to make light of the situation and assure him that I'm okay with whatever this is and whatever we are. "Yes. Your dad was telling me about his life in the Marine Corps. Very exciting. Did you know he was a 'Hollywood Marine'?"

"Yep. He went through training in San Diego as compared to South Carolina." Michael slowly stands and says, "Semper fi. Well, I'll leave you both to catch up. I have an early morning."

"Do you need a ride?" I ask. "I have rounds to do at the hospital tomorrow morning and can drop you if you're headed in that direction."

The conflict is evident in his eyes and body language, but I don't want to push. "No. I can get a ride in the morning."

He walks upstairs, leaving Cameron and me sitting on the patio listening to the quiet. "Would you like a glass of shiraz?" I offer.

"No, thanks. I'm pretty tired." He winks at me. "There's this fiery redhead who's been keeping me up recently."

My need for him grows as I stare at my empty wineglass. "I could use company tonight, but I have a feeling you have some things to manage upstairs in your place."

"He always wants something from me."

"I don't want to get into the middle, but…."

"Good, then don't." His eyes are set, his voice firm.

His response is curt and a bit hurtful. I'm sure he's struggling with his dad's illness though, so I won't hold it against him. "Cameron, he's spent the last two hours telling me how proud he is of you."

"Don't insert yourself in this, Hadlee," he warns as he gets up from the table and storms upstairs.

I understand that it isn't my place to tell Cameron how bad his dad's diagnosis may be, but I hope they can work this out. I want to take him by the hand and lead him away. I want to walk with him, talk with him, but he has a solid wall that he isn't interested in my breaking it down.

Even if we don't remain lovers, he's still my friend, a kindred spirit. I just want to tell him that I'm here for him.

chapter TWENTY

CAMERON

THE TENSION IS HIGH WITH HADLEE after my unreasonable outburst over my dad. He just fucks everything up. This morning he called and asked to stay a few days, and I'm allowing him. I don't want to, but something's up, and he doesn't seem to want to tell me. I'm angry with him and have been for a very long time. I know I should extend an olive branch instead of hostility, but sometimes it isn't easy with my dad, and now he's put Hadlee in the middle of our mess.

I'd like things to go back to how things were before he arrived. Peaceful.

I'm lost in my thoughts when my cell phone pings.

Mason: Please join me at my place at 7 tonight. Big news.

Dillon sticks his head in my office. "Do you have any idea what the 'Big News' is?"

"No idea, but if he's telling us he's proposing to Annabel, I'm voting we remove his partnership."

"I think it's something else. Did you drive today?"

"No. I took a Lyft into the office," I tell him.

"Emerson and Greer will meet us at Mason's, and Sara and

Cynthia will ride over with us. Meet by the elevators at six thirty?"

"Okay. See you then."

I spend what's left of the afternoon concentrating on my work. Or at least trying. Something always brings me back to Hadlee and a pink handprint on her perfect ivory derrière. The thought of her bound with nipple clamps makes my dick hard.

As we all pile into Dillon's SUV, the girls sit in the back, and I sit with Dillon in the front. We spend the short drive to the top of Nob Hill discussing all the reasons Mason could be summoning us. We all agree that if he's proposing to Annabel, we'll bring in Charles and the lawyers. Other than that, no one has any clue as to why he's called the meeting.

Dillon finds a parking space a few blocks from Mason's and we walk over. As we arrive, Charles and Trey are being dropped by a car service ahead of us, and Emerson, CeCe, and Greer pull in behind us. It seems like the gang's all here.

CeCe leans in and says, "If Mason has proposed to Annabel, I'm leaving."

Emerson places her hand on CeCe's shoulder. "Cameron agrees. Don't you worry."

Again I'm reminded of how Mason missed the boat with CeCe. She would be a great match for him. *What a mess.* We're buzzed in and walk back to Mason's place, where we're greeted by his dog Misty.

Mason walks up behind Misty, patting her head. "Hey, guys. Thanks for coming at the last minute. There are beers and wine out in the courtyard."

Annabel is nowhere to be seen. That's a good sign. However, I'm surprised when I spot our private investigator, Jim.

Mason has set up his patio with enough chairs so we all can sit while we wait to find out why we've been summoned. I take a beer and watch. Everyone seems anxious to hear what they've learned.

Once everyone is settled, Jim begins. "Well, Quinn at Perkins Klein has shared some things going on within the company." Quinn is a longtime friend of SHN and ex-girlfriend of Mason. We reached out to her to find out what she knew about how they were getting our information. We weren't looking for who they were bidding on, but rather for information that would protect our assets and use it as a countermeasure to discover who's feeding Perkins Klein all our confidential information.

We all stare at him expectantly, and he continues. "Financially, they're struggling. They're firing a few highly paid members of their various teams rather than doing layoffs. They're being blamed for the bad investments."

"Well, that's no surprise," Mason says, and we all agree.

"Now here's the interesting part," Jim states. "Quinn is pretty tight with Bob Perkins and Terry Klein, and in the mess of Terry going into the hospital, it was shared that she didn't think they would be getting the insider information for much longer. It sounded to Quinn like they didn't know who was behind the leak on our team."

"What does that mean? Is someone leaving piles of our information on their doorstep?" I ask.

"Well, I think they're getting the information by e-mail, but they're blind e-mail accounts."

"If it isn't Perkins Klein behind this breach, why would anyone go to this length to sabotage us?"

With a whistle, Dillon says, "Fuck. This could mean starting all over."

"Exactly," Jim agrees.

Mason sits forward in his chair. "Wait. Someone else may be behind this?"

"That's what we're beginning to think."

"What would you advise for our next steps?" Sara asks.

Looking around the group, Jim says, "This is extremely personal. Someone is going after you where it hurts. Any thoughts from you? Maybe someone you didn't invest in and they're blaming you?"

"We get thousands of asks a year," Dillon replies. "That would be tough to track, but I can get you a comprehensive list. How far back do you want to go?"

"As far back as you can give us."

Dillon nods and gets on his phone, tapping rapidly.

Turning to me, Jim asks, "This may be ignorance on my part, but how often do you get similar proposals that only vary by technology?"

"We try to stay away from those that are essentially the same idea with different technology approaches. We tend to favor more unique concepts," I tell him.

Jim crosses his arms and thinks a few moments. "Okay, has anyone ever accused you of stealing or sharing their technology?"

"We've had a few disgruntled applicants. I have a file here on my laptop." After a few clicks, Sara looks up and says, "You have the file in your inbox. In it are multiple documents with a few that have some legal proceedings attached."

"Good." Turning to Emerson, he asks, "Has anyone on your

team mentioned anything about a client who's unhappy with you?"

"No. I haven't heard anything."

"Would they tell you if they did hear anything?"

Emerson thinks a moment. "I believe so. If their client's unhappy with us, it typically means they'll be out of a job, so they want things fixed."

"Cynthia, Greer, this mess started before the two of you joined the firm, but you have fresh eyes. Any thoughts?"

Both girls shake their heads and say, "No," in unison.

"What do you think our next steps should be?" Charles asks Jim.

"I think we should sit with each of you and get into some of your histories to see if we can uncover something in your personal lives. From there, we may determine if we should meet with your teams."

We talk for a while longer and order Chinese takeout as we dissect who it could be, including a woman I ghosted last year when I learned she was dating someone else. She was pretty upset that I wasn't interested in her leaving her boyfriend for me.

My personal life's a mess with my dad. Things are not pretty with Hadlee right now, and this shit at work's a giant clusterfuck.

Why can't one thing go right?

chapter
TWENTY-ONE

HADLEE

I STOP BY MY HOUSE on my way home from work. The construction is going so slow. I'm grateful that Cameron put a call into the insurance company and they agreed to pay for the reconstruction, so now I have a contractor, but they haven't done much.

I spoke with the architect, and we discussed some potential changes to the house. I'm putting in a bay window in the front room which will add some curb appeal, and we're redesigning the kitchen. I'm excited to finally have a kitchen for someone who cooks.

As I look around the black cavern that was once my living room, they've barely begun gutting the debris or pulling down the wall between the dining room and kitchen. It doesn't look like they've done much more than cover the hole in the ceiling.

If Cameron and I were talking, I'd ask him to put a call in to the contractor and see if he couldn't get him to move along. But we really aren't talking, so that isn't going to happen.

I want my house back. I'll miss being so close to Cameron, but I think I may be overstaying my welcome.

Why is it that these guys won't move when a woman asks them, but bring in a six-foot-four man and they jump right to it?

I WORK FOUR DAYS A WEEK, which usually means I have Fridays off. I'm all packed to meet the girls for our weekend in Napa.

I haven't spoken to Cameron all week. I guess we've moved to "friends who occasionally enjoy playing together naked." A little voice in my head reminds me that sleeping with my landlord was a mistake, but I can't help but be a little bit disappointed. We get along well when we're wearing clothes, after, so it isn't only my body craving his touch.

CeCe picks me up on her way to get Emerson and Greer. Unfortunately, Sara can't join us. She's doing some destination wedding planning with CeCe's mom and her foster mom. She was so sweet to ask me to be in the wedding, but I'm afraid I'll always be the bridesmaid and never the bride.

I'm just feeling sorry for myself is all. I want to tell my friends how disappointed I am, but he's their friend and coworker, and I don't want them to feel like they have to choose between the two of us. I'm going to pick myself up off the proverbial floor and pretend my body doesn't ache for his touch.

As I load my suitcase in CeCe's Land Rover, I climb in next to her. With a twinkle in her eye, she asks, "You look wonderful. You have a glow about you. Anything new going on you wish to share?"

Chuckling, I tell her, "Nothing new. The house is under construction, and I'm still boring."

We pick up Emerson and Greer from their office and then head north into Napa, talking about our jobs, our love lives, and fashion. My favorite subjects.

CeCe randomly asks, "What the hell's going on with Mason and Annabel?"

"I know, right? Apparently Mason told Sara that Annabel would be moving in with him, but she needs to find another job first," Emerson shares.

"Good grief. Really? Moving in? That's too bad," I tell them.

"Well on the positive side, it would take the prospect of a sexual harassment suit off the table if she were to find another job that was better than the one she has now."

"What's she qualified for?"

"Looking pretty and snagging a rich man," CeCe retorts.

Emerson snorts. We're getting rowdy, and we haven't even had a glass of wine yet. "No shit," Greer exclaims.

"Then it's safe to assume she's a firecracker in bed," I comment. "How come I can't snag a good guy? I think I'm pretty decent in bed." In an attempt to be funny, I put my hands beneath my breasts and lift them up. "And talk about a pair of knockers."

"I'm pretty jealous of those," CeCe chimes in. "You've been turning heads for years, and I've been your faithful sidekick."

"I don't think you're anyone's sidekick," Emerson says.

CeCe glances in her rearview mirror at us. "I hate to break it to you, but with her rack, we're all sidekicks."

"I'd happily give them to you. I'd give you all some. They attract too much attention. My back hurts, and I can't sleep on my stomach. I'll give you half, even."

We all giggle at that.

"Hadlee, how are things going with Cameron?" Greer asks.

I internally cringe. I hate that we aren't more. "He's dealing with his dad, and he's a good landlord."

"Wait, I thought you were hanging out with him last weekend?"

"Not really. He took me for a ride in his Porsche. He's becoming a good friend."

CeCe pouts. "You didn't tell me he took you for a ride. The big question I have is if it's friends with benefits."

I hate that I want to lie to my friends, but I don't want the extra questions or to explain how our sex life has a slight naughty bend to it. Since his father's arrival, there's been a distance. I understand why, but I need to protect myself from getting hurt. "No, just tenant and landlord."

As we make the winding drive from Highway 1 into Napa, I stare at the acres after acres of vineyards as far as the eye can see. This area is uniquely California, and it's so beautiful as we head through the towns next to the rolling hills of grapes.

I don't want to talk about Cameron. He's still giving me the silent treatment for asking about his dad. I hear his dad occasionally, and sometimes I'll spot him on the patio, so I know he's still around. It makes me wonder if he's told Cameron that he's sick.

I just need to put it all behind me and enjoy my time with my friends.

We arrive at the Meadowood Spa and Resort. It's my birthday weekend, and I'm excited to get away. CeCe always makes a big deal about my birthday because she knows it's also the anniversary of my mother's death.

Meadowood is a stunning five-star resort in the middle of Napa. Rather than a hotel, it's covered with small chalets with multiple themes and is a pure oasis a short distance from the hustle and bustle of San Francisco. My favorite is the spa. We have several treatments planned this weekend, and I can't wait.

When we arrive, they call CeCe by name. She's made reservations for us in two of the Hillside Majestic chalets. They're two-bedroom chalets, and I'm staying with CeCe. We're given driving directions to our specific cabins, and the footmen meet us as we arrive to move our luggage to our rooms.

Standing at the grand window, the views are spectacular. CeCe hands me a cup of tea. "It must've been super difficult for you at work these past few weeks. Diagnosing a child with a terminal illness must be so devastating. And I haven't forgotten all you've been through with the fire, but remember our goal is to pamper ourselves. I got you this weekend. This is your birthday present. Please don't let everything going on at home keep you from enjoying your weekend."

I give her a big hug. "CeCe, I'm not sure what I would do if I didn't have you."

"Greer, Emerson, and Sara would take great care of you."

"Not like you do. Thank you for being such a wonderful friend and sister from another mother. I still make a decent living, and I can swing things this weekend."

"I know you can, but this weekend is for your birthday—and setting up Greer with Andy."

"She's going to love him. He's handsome and seems perfect for her. We're heading over later this afternoon?"

"Yes. We have our first round of spa treatments after brunch. We should be nicely relaxed by that point, and then Meadowood's shuttle will meet us at three to take us over. Don't tell Greer, but I've asked Andy to personally give us a tour of his vineyard."

"Does he realize you're trying to fix him up?"

"I'll never tell," she says with a smirk.

"I think it'll be pretty obvious what you're up to, CeCe."

"Don't worry, missy. I have my eye on someone for you, too."

"I think I need to focus on work and me for a while."

"I understand." She gives me another big hug. "Finish your tea and let's get over and start enjoying the amenities of the spa. I want to delight in the relaxation gardens and dip in the mineral pool before I get my facial and seaweed wrap."

"I'm excited about the private spa suites. All those fragrant soaps, oils, and lotions to enjoy? I must warn you, I may be jelly by the time I get to Andy's."

"And jelly's what you deserve to be." CeCe gives me an encouraging squeeze.

I reach into my suitcase and pull out my cosmetics bag, the outfit that Jennifer at Nordstrom's pulled together for me, and the bikini I wore in Colorado. I'm ready to go. We won't be returning to our room until after dinner this evening, and we'll get ready in the Zen of the spa for our afternoon and evening.

Meadowood is known for having private suites for their guests of the spa for treatments, or you can sit in saunas with friends and enjoy time with others. I carry stress in my back, so getting the knots worked out of it is my first priority.

I have fifteen minutes before my massage, so I walk into my suite and enjoy the view of rolling green hills filled with various grape vines and fruit orchards. Unpacking my dress for the evening, I hang it up on a hook in the huge bathroom. Staring at the jetted tub, I can't wait to use the bath bombs I ordered after my massage.

Soft sounds of running water can be heard over speakers. Undressing, I put on the plush terry cloth robe and feel the relaxation beginning. The stress of the fire, challenges at work, my stepmother's mess, and the absence of Cameron in my sex life floats away, leaving me serene and content.

There's a knock at the door, and the concierge peeks in. "Ms. Ford, Raul, your therapist, will be here in a few short minutes. I have your sheet here. He's to work on knots in your back, and you're good with lavender oil. Anything else?"

I shake my head. "No."

"Do you need anything before he arrives?"

"No, thank you. I should be all set."

Lying facedown, I rest my face in a cradle and a pillow under my shoulders to take the pressure off my breasts. I'm naked under the covers as I listen to the rainfall sounds coming from the speakers. My mind is busy and moving like a pinball stuck between bumpers. I concentrate on my breathing, and slowly the tension eases.

There's another soft knock and Raul enters. Through the cradle, I can tell he's lowered the lights. "Ms. Ford, I understand you would like some extra attention paid to your upper back. Please let me know if the pressure becomes too much."

I smell the sweet scent of the lavender filling the air as I hear the squish of oil squeezed from a bottle. His first touch is gentle, and his hands are warm, the massage oil allowing them to glide smoothly over my bare skin. Moving around my back, he works from a slow, soothing massage with light pressure to a more vigorous treatment. When it comes to my upper back, Raul uses firm pressure throughout the massage, warming the tissue up and then applying pressure in a slow and focused way, coaxing the muscles and knots to release. At times it's sharp, though not painful, but once the knots release, there is a sigh of relief. I'm so relaxed I vacillate between a light slumber and total relaxation. It's ninety minutes of pure ecstasy.

When Raul finishes, he quietly says, "Please take your time getting up. You have a large glass of water to drink, and please consider a bath in the jetted tub. If you need anything, the concierge can get it and have it delivered to your room."

I hear the door to my suite open and close as Raul exits, and I'm slow to sit up, completely relaxed and content. Slowly I move into the bathroom and start the warm water in the tub. It fills quickly, and I turn the jets on. When I drop in two bath bombs, the room is filled with the smell of lavender and a hint of vanilla. Resting my head back, I snooze slightly. I don't think about work, my house fire, or Cameron. My mind and body are relaxed, and I only get out of the tub because the water has become tepid and I'm beginning to get cold.

Glancing at the clock, I have about an hour before it's time to leave. I use liberal amounts of lotion and begin the process of getting ready for our winery visit and eventually dinner.

CeCe and I have a favorite winery—Bellissima Valle, which is only three years into making wine. Andy Giordano owns the vineyard along with his family. He comes from an Italian winemaking family, and he brought grapes from his family vineyards in Italy and Argentina. Napa's warm summers and temperate winters make the grapes perfect for great red wines. We make arrangements with Meadowood's car service to be dropped at the vineyard, the car staying to wait for us unless another guest calls We can always get a ride back with Lyft if the happens.

CeCe and I found Bellissima Valle on accident. One of my friends from residency had shared a winery she liked when she'd been wandering around St. Helena in Napa Valley. It was new, and she kept calling it "undiscovered." We decided to try to find it. I can be a bit directionally challenged, and CeCe's always a good sport to tag along to visit a winery on a Saturday afternoon. We followed a winding road until we topped a crest and looked across the acres of grapes. It was so beautiful, and sitting in the center was this winery surrounded by wide olive trees and large warehouses that look like giant metal barns.

Maybe it called to us because of the Italian influence rather than the French, which is often found in Napa, but we found ourselves at Bellissima. We could see the Tuscan-style villa from the road, and the tasting room signs inviting us to join them seemed to call to us, so we stopped.

Exiting CeCe's Land Rover, we walked across the gravel driveway into what looked like an old farmhouse imported from Italy. We loved it at first sight. When we entered the room, a gentleman came over and immediately introduced himself in a thick Italian accent as Andrea, but to call him Andy. He was preparing to close for the day, but he poured us two glasses of his favorite wine and chatted with us for over an hour about his passion for wine and the business.

We were in love with Bellissima from that moment on. CeCe and I have been here often and bought a lot of wine from them ever since.

Driving over the rain-kissed streets, my breath is once again taken away by the views of the grapes. Bellissima is becoming more popular. I'm happy that people are discovering them, but nothing beats the exclusivity of our first visit. When we walk in, the tasting room's busy, but CeCe spots our regular table and sits down.

Sophia, Andy's sister, walks up with her arms open. "*La mia bella* CeCe!"

CeCe stands to greet her, and they hug and kiss on each cheek. She turns and introduces everyone to Sophia, and we each order the red flight of tastings—the merlot, cabernet sauvignon, and a red blend.

"I'm impressed with how busy you are," CeCe tells her.

"Oh, I know. We couldn't give this away two years ago, and now we have certain wines people are buying futures for."

"Future years?" Emerson asks. "How far ahead?" She blushes after asking the personal question. "I'm mean, if I wanted to buy the wine, how far in the future would I be buying?"

"It's okay. We require a case purchase, and we're close to selling out two years from now and will soon move to three."

Emerson turns to Greer. "Now I understand your passion for wine as a business."

Sophia turns to retrieve our wine, and we're left to take in the tasting room. It's dimly lit, making me feel as if I'm in the heart of a wine cellar. The walls are covered in rows of large wooden casks, each marked with a grape type and a year. These casks are all from last year. It blows my mind that they've come to use their tasting room as storage and are selling futures. I'm happy for Andy and his sister that they've become such a success.

The room sports maybe a dozen tables, each one full of guests drinking samples, and people are standing at the bar speaking with the staff member who pours the wine.

As we finish our tasting, Andy arrives open-armed. In a thick Italian accent, he draws out, "CeCe," then hugs her and kisses her on both cheeks. Turning to me, he does the same. "Hadlee, you're more beautiful each time I see you."

CeCe turns to introduce the rest of our group. "Andy, I'd like you to meet Emerson. It was her wedding that we shipped your wine to."

"Benvenuta, bella signora. Sono incantato di conoscerla." He hugs and kisses Emerson on each cheek.

"Thank you. The wine was delicious."

"This is our good friend Greer," CeCe continues.

Turning to her, he says, *"Bella mia,* you're absolutely the most beautiful creature I've ever seen."

Biting her lip, she flirts, "You're quite the charmer, aren't you?"

No one feature makes Andy handsome, though his eyes come close. People often speak of the dark chocolate color of eyes, as if that were of importance, yet he would be beautiful in any shade. From them comes an intensity, an honesty, a gentleness. As each year passes, the lines will deepen upon his face, and he'll be more handsome still, as if his soul shines through his skin. He has the kind of face that stops you in your tracks. I guess he must get used to that.

As we're all sharing our thoughts on our tasting with Andy, I notice a blonde woman with big hair and fake boobs try to get his attention. Her behavior suggests she's used to getting her way. Andy may see her but doesn't pay attention if he does. Her frustration evident, she interrupts us. "Andy, dahling, I hope you'll consider joining us tonight at the French Laundry. I know Thomas Keller personally and told him you might stop by, and he assured me that he would make room for you." Her nonchalant gaze and a weak smile give away her insecurity.

Andy blushes, a dead giveaway that he isn't comfortable with aggressive women. It doesn't help that he's so modest with his beauty; it makes the girls fall for him faster and harder. He's handsome all right, but inside he's beautiful, and I can tell that Greer's absolutely smitten with him already. "Thank you, my friend, but as I said before, I have plans this evening." He winks at Greer. "Please enjoy your evening with Thomas. Give him my best. The food is incredible."

The strange woman walks away, obviously disappointed, and I watch her get in a black Ferrari before pulling recklessly out of the parking lot onto the street.

Apologizing to us, he says, "I'm so sorry, my lovelies. I understand you ladies would like a tour of my vineyard?"

"Yes, please," CeCe replies.

"Well, come with me behind the proverbial curtain." He opens a door and leads us outside to his fields of vines. "Here at Bellissima Valle, we have over five hundred acres of vines. Making wine is a long, slow process. It can take a full three years to get from the initial planting of a brand-new grapevine through the first harvest, and the first vintage might not be bottled for another two years after that. But when soil and sunlight along with climate combine with winemaking skill, the finished product's worth the wait.

"These vines to your right are our merlot grapes. They're the first I planted almost ten years ago. We have pinot noir, merlot, and malbec vines in this area. A few acres of the petite sirah and finally"—he motions to the far east of his property—"we have over a hundred acres of cabernet sauvignon."

Greer is obviously amazed, her mouth gaping. "How many acres have you planted?"

"We're a medium-size vineyard with roughly one thousand acres."

I'm stunned. "How many bottles of wine does that produce per year?"

"Well, we get between eight and ten tons of grapes per acre, and on a decent year, it takes one ton of grapes to produce a little more than two barrels of wine. Each barrel contains about sixty gallons, which is twenty-five cases or three hundred bottles. So, one ton of grapes yields about sixty cases, or seven hundred and twenty bottles."

We're all awestruck. Greer, visibly impressed, asks, "What's your sales channel?"

"We're luckier than most, as we have a following from our vines in Italy, France, Germany, and South America, so we've been selling well enough to keep our creditors at bay, but when we're at capacity, we'll go to more high-end wine shops."

He and Greer have a technical winemaking conversation as he leads us to an extended golf cart and drives us to where the real winemaking takes place in a giant warehouse on the property. It's a temperature-controlled area stacked to the ceiling with row after row of barrels of wine. There must be several hundred barrels with signs above that have a grape type and year.

I'm stunned. I knew there was a lot of work between the grape and bottling, but not like this. "Wow. What a huge operation."

"It didn't start out this way, but over time and several bank loans, we've grown. Maybe one day we'll make a profit, but I love this business. It's in my blood. The wine has been likened to 'poetry in a bottle.'"

Greer's lips quirk, and she shares with him, "Just like any creative process, winemaking requires knowledge, commitment, and time."

Andy lights up, and if I was a betting woman, I'd guess he was just as smitten with Greer.

We pull up in front of the tasting room at the end of our tour. It's beginning to close for the evening, and he gets out some specific bottles for us to sample from the vineyards in Italy and Argentina. "How do these compare?"

Greer beams. "I can tell the maturity of the vineyard. I smell some vanilla and peach in the notes. It lingers appropriately on my palate. Truly a wonderful wine."

"Is there any chance of ordering some of these bottles?" CeCe asks.

"Unfortunately, we only sell futures for these vintages."

I'm still surprised by people paying for something and not getting it for at least another year. Not wanting to appear dumb, I ask, "What's the futures timeline for these wines?"

"We have more buyers than wine, so right now we're selling seven seasons from now."

"I'll take a case," CeCe says. Turning to me, she shares, "We can split it."

I nod in agreement.

Andy collects all our information and then helps us load eight cases and a few odd bottles into the trunk of the Meadowood car. It's a tight fit, but we manage.

"What a glorious afternoon," Greer dreamily says.

Andy hugs and kisses us each on both cheeks, lingering a bit with Greer, then waves goodbye as we drive away in the Meadowood shuttle.

WE HAVE DINNER PLANS on property at The Restaurant at Meadowood. It's a Michelin three-star-rated restaurant, which normally I would pass on—too expensive for one meal—but I want to splurge this weekend. Dinner will run over $500 a person. I normally don't spend that kind of money on something as disposable as food, but it is my birthday, after all. Plus, as I turn another year older and my biological clock is ticking louder and louder each day, I can't help but feel a bit heartbroken by Cameron. I would love to explore something with him, but my brief conversation with his dad still has him avoiding me.

The dining room's a sophisticated barn of sorts, decked with polished stone tables, wood columns, and rural splendor. It makes for an elegant backdrop for romantic evenings for our girls' weekend, as long as we don't get too rowdy and interrupt the other patrons.

This is a serious restaurant for the true foody, and I'm in heaven. It doesn't seat many people, which gives the impression of an intimate dinner. The maître d' greets us by name as we arrive and shows us to a private dining room overlooking the courtyard lit by flame torches. As he holds my chair for me and then places the napkin on my lap, he says, "Happy birthday, Miss

Hadlee. We are so pleased that you are sharing your birthday weekend with us. The chef has prepared a few surprises for you."

The Restaurant at Meadowood offers a tasting menu or a regular one, which they call the "Counter Menu." Tonight's rack of lamb or the cod as the main course sound too good to pass up, so we all agree to go with the five-course meal on the tasting menu. CeCe has brought with her several bottles of various wines of Bellissima Valle's reserved wine for us to enjoy with a corkage fee.

"Dillon is so jealous that we're eating here," Emerson exclaims. "We had such a great meal a few years ago at the French Laundry. I'm sure this will be at least as good."

"I love them both equally," CeCe confides.

As we enjoy our meals and rehash our day at the spa and touring Bellissima, I turn to Greer and ask, "So, what did you think of Andy?"

She grins wide and says, "There's no doubt that he's handsome."

We all nod and talk about his dreamy chocolate-brown eyes, gorgeous dark hair, and the broad shoulders to match.

"But I don't think he was interested in me."

CeCe appears shocked. "What do you mean?"

"Remember that strange woman in the tasting room?"

We all nod and say in unison, "Yes."

"Well, he was just as polite to her as he was with us."

CeCe huffs. "I don't know about that. He didn't offer to show her the grounds."

"CeCe, you have bought many cases of wine from him for your business, Emerson's wedding, and yourself. You're a good customer," Greer implores. "He didn't really talk to me. He was very good at flirting with all of us equally."

CeCe seems disappointed. "You both spent a lot of time talking about wines, and I thought when you said the bit about wine being a creative process that he was going to bend you over the table and take you right there."

"You're funny. I think he was good with customer service. I like him, and there's a small spark, but I don't think there was a lightning bolt."

Not to be deterred, CeCe asks, "Well, if he were to ask for your phone number, could I give it to him?"

"Sure. But don't offer unless he asks."

I lean in to Greer and pat her arm. "Honey, we've talked to Andy many times. We thought you'd both like each other. If you don't like him, that's fine. We'll put CeCe's yenta matchmaker hat on and put her back to work."

She smiles. "Honestly, I don't know if I'm ready to date." Greer dated Mark for eight years, but he dumped her a little over a year ago for another woman who he felt was a better political match and had less family baggage than Greer.

CeCe cuts in. "Mark was an asshole. He will go nowhere in politics if I have anything to say about it."

"And he has a little dick, too." Greer holds up her pinky finger and flexes it for us to see and laugh hysterically.

"You deserve much better than that," Emerson shares.

As I glance around the room, I note that all the servers are impeccable, professional, and understand how to keep their guests happy and at ease. Our water and wineglasses are never empty, and they seem to have a sixth sense to know what we want before we do. It almost seems as if there are more servers than diners.

Our first course arrives, and it's a wonderfully fragrant abalone, wild onion, and bean soup. I can taste a hint of butter, but the abalone is what makes this a wonderful take on onion soup. The sommelier pairs it with the Italian chardonnay, which is a crisp and perfect complement. I come up just short of licking the bowl, it tastes so wonderful.

Turning to Emerson, I ask, "Do you think they serve seconds?"

She giggles. "Possibly, if you want more."

"This probably is one of those soups that is more a minute on the lips, forever on the hips," I muse. They roll up a cart, and it's mesmerizing to watch them make the salad course next to the table. This is something they're famous for—eggplant foster, a vegetable take on bananas foster. The server informs us that the beautiful small purple fruit is grown fresh and was picked today from the garden in the back. We watch them pan fry the eggplant in butter, adding rum and a liqueur before the server places several pieces of the eggplant on a bed of endive leaves of lettuce and a generous portion of mascarpone cheese. Spooning lavish amounts of the liqueur upon the dish, they light it on fire for a stunning display that burns itself out shortly after being placed in front of each of us.

Taking my first bite, my senses are overwhelmed by the perfect balance of fresh and exotic.

Greer moans her satisfaction as Emerson leans over to me. "This is pure food orgasm."

"Incredible," CeCe agrees.

Recovering from our food enchantment, our conversation

moves to fashion. CeCe is the CEO for the makeup manufacturer Metro Composition Cosmetics, and she shares, “We’re so excited. Metro Composition has been asked by three major designers to do the makeup for Fashion Week in New York.”

This is huge for CeCe, especially since a percentage of the profits her company makes goes back into women’s charities. She’s been working on landing Fashion Week for years. “Are you serious? You’ve wanted to do this forever. Why didn’t you tell us you were working on this?”

Very dramatically, CeCe says, “Oh, we’re always working on something.” Leaning in so no one around us can hear, she whispers, “And besides, not everyone wants to work with us. We aren’t a big name.”

“You could sell to the big cosmetic companies, but you love that you make a difference,” Greer chides her.

“Will you be the makeup artist?” Emerson asks.

“No way. I’ll be there and in and out of the various shows. I believe I’ll get extra tickets. Anyone want to join me?”

We all give her an enthusiastic “Yes!”

“I’ll include Sara, and I like Cynthia, the new partner at SHN. Maybe she’ll want to come, too?”

“She’d be crazy not to,” Greer declares.

The staff has cleared our plates and poured Bellissima's pinot from Argentina. I take my first sip and immediately fall in love with this wine. It sits nicely on my palate, not too fruity or bitter. “Wow. I think this is my favorite Bellissima wine yet.”

Greer takes several small sips and pronounces, “I like it.”

CeCe giggles. “You’re funny.”

Cupping her hair from the bottom and turning to gaze over

her shoulder while channeling Marilyn Monroe, Greer breathlessly croons, "Why thank you."

The staff arrives with our dinner. Placed in front of me are the most glorious lamb chops with roasted pluot, finished before our eyes with a copper pot of marigold-coriander jus. I hate to disrupt the beauty of the plate, but my taste buds are screaming for me to start. It's pure heaven, the soft flavors of cauliflower custard topped with caviar nearly exploding in my mouth. The hint of mint and a spice I can't place combine to create perfection.

CeCe has the cod main course with roasted cabbage and oysters with a nettles sauce. She offers me a bite, and it's also incredible. She tries my lamb and nods enthusiastically with a big "Mmm." She calls the server over and says, "Please share with Chef Pierre that every course has progressively gotten better. Truly a fantastic meal."

"Thank you, Miss CeCe. I will be sure to tell him. Would you like him to come out to the table?"

"We'd love that, but make sure he knows he can come only if he has time."

The server nods and pours more wine into each of our glasses.

CeCe leans over and says, "It's not over yet, birthday girl."

I blush. "Everything's been perfect."

We sit for a short time, our private room reserved for the evening so we can enjoy the time together uninterrupted. Dessert is a wonderful tart with exotic fruit and berries from their orchards and gardens. Mine is placed last with a giant sparkler, and the room fills with what seems like the entire restaurant staff. The lights dim while the chef and CeCe lead all who've gathered in singing "Happy Birthday."

The sparkler gives the room a beautiful muted appearance as I gaze at my collection of friends and the very kind staff of the restaurant. My life is almost perfect. I'm grateful for so many things. I miss my mom so much this time of year, but I'm lucky to have these people who love me unconditionally.

I feel as if I'm only missing one thing. Closing my eyes tightly, I wish for Cameron to be here with me, too.

In a beautiful French accent, Chef Pierre croons, "May all your dreams come true."

I enjoy every last bite of the delicate custard and crisp assortment of fruit. It takes all of my willpower to not lick the plate clean.

"Thank you. Dinner was perfect." I can't help but grin from ear to ear and try to keep the tears at bay.

CeCe and Greer gush about their meals, and Emerson grabs my hand below the table and gives me a warm squeeze, whispering, "Happy birthday, sweetie. I do hope your wish includes a man who adores you."

I smile. "I hope so, too."

I don't even notice the check placed discreetly at CeCe's elbow until Emerson and Greer each hand her their credit card. I attempt to pull mine from my purse, when Greer declares, "Oh no. Don't even think about it. This is our treat."

I try to convince them it isn't necessary, that it's too extravagant, but the girls split the bill three ways, paying for my dinner. It's incredibly sweet of them, and I'm overwhelmed by the generosity of my friends.

chapter TWENTY-TWO

HADLEE

SLOWLY AND RELUCTANTLY, I uncover my face. I blink, close my eyes, and blink again. Streaks of sunlight penetrate the window and blind me. My brain is in overdrive.

Sitting up, I drag my feet off the bed and rub the sleep from my eyes, then stretch my arms above my head and yawn. My legs dangle above the sparkling golden wood floors, the fatigue of everything going on in my life slowly seeping out of me as the goldfinches chirp their morning greeting. Eventually, I get out of bed and stumble across to the other side of the chalet in search of coffee.

Waking up can be harsh, especially if your dreams are better than reality. In my dreams, I have my house as it was before the fire and a loving relationship with Cameron. The saddest part of it is that eventually, the memory of my dream fades—if I'm even lucky enough to remember it. In place of my dreams come my daydreams. Because without those daydreams, I'm left with this lonely feeling of detachment and the reality of the empty void of emotions, the only proof I ever had of the dream to begin with.

Spotting the Keurig, I absently pop a random K-cup under the spigot and press the button. The smell draws me in and helps my brain catch up with my mind as the machine produces a full-bodied cup of coffee. Taking my first sip, I murmur, "Ahh, the nectar of the gods." Today is going to be perfect. I will it so.

It's Saturday morning, and it's quiet. The dew adds another color to the natural greens of the landscape, punctuated by a pair of squirrels playing what seems like a game of tag as they chase each other up and down the trees.

We purposely didn't plan much today; it's a day on our own for pool, spa, and sleep. I have a facial scheduled and a massage this afternoon, a nice but naughty book on my Kindle, and we have dinner plans. More birthday celebrations.

We agreed to meet at our chalet before going out as a group for dinner. Jennifer found me a beautiful rose-colored dress for tonight, the neck giving me a subtle hint of cleavage below the ruffle as it drapes my shoulder. The length is demure and sits just below my knee with a seductive slit up to my mid-thigh. It's the perfect mix of conservative and sexy. Underneath I have matching bra and pantie set that, while beautiful, is more about function than sex. Slipping into a sexy strappy gold stiletto sandal, I stand and stare at myself in the mirror.

Today is the day I'm actually thirty-three years old. The same age my mother was when she was diagnosed with her cancer, and she died twenty-four years ago today. I hear CeCe and the girls in the other room, and it sounds like everyone's here. I don't want to wallow in my self-pity, and I don't want to cry and ruin my makeup, but I always wish my mom was here to hug me and celebrate another milestone. I also miss my dad, who died a few years ago, but we weren't close after my mom died, so I find that I tend to miss her more.

Gathering my courage to make it through my evening without my mom or dad, I grab my pearl-adorned clutch and walk into the main room to join my friends. With each step, my head is higher, and my smile becomes my façade.

"Here she is!" Greer exclaims.

CeCe pops a bottle of champagne, pours everyone a glass, and hands it to each of us. We all raise our glasses as she begins her toast. "Wishing you a happy, healthy, and incredible year ahead. May all your dreams come true."

We clink our glasses together, and everyone shouts, "Here, here."

"Are we ready for a fun night?" CeCe asks.

I nod, and Emerson says, "We were born ready."

We make the short walk over to the Meadowood main area, and I expect to get in a car for a drive to whatever restaurant we have reservations for. I'm not paying attention when we're shown to a private dining room. I'm led in first, and the room is dark. I think for a moment that I've gone to the wrong area and I stop short. Suddenly the lights come on, the room stuffed full of my friends, who, in unison, all yell, "Surprise!"

I think my heart stops. Glancing around the room, there must be over a hundred people here, and hanging from the ceiling is a large banner saying I'm twenty-nine and holding for the fourth year. I'm stunned and speechless.

I turn to gape at CeCe. Smiling from ear to ear, she mouths to me, "Surprise. I love you." I want to cry because I'm overwhelmed by her generosity and for being such a great friend, but before I can do that, people are crowding in to hug me and give me personal birthday congratulations.

Friend after friend asks, "Were you surprised?" To those, I say, "Completely! I had no idea. This is my best birthday ever."

For those who share, "I almost slipped and told you when...," I reply, "This is completely unexpected. Thank you so much for joining me to celebrate."

It takes better than an hour before Cameron comes over. He's so handsome in his khaki pants, a nice pair of light brown suede derby shoes, and a blue and white checked cotton button-down shirt with a white T-shirt underneath. His hair is slicked back, and he looks good enough to eat. Our chemistry is undeniable. He runs his finger up my arms and whispers, "Hey, sweet thing. Happy birthday."

His seductive voice makes my stomach flip and my panties wet. "Hey, Cameron. Thanks for coming."

"I wouldn't have missed this for the world." He grins at me, and I swear he's like a cat who just caught the canary.

I lick my lips at the hooded desire in his eyes. "Are you staying here in Napa tonight?"

He nods. "Yes. I don't want to drink and drive, so I found a small room not far from here at a bed-and-breakfast. You seemed surprised by the party."

"I didn't expect it at all. CeCe didn't hint or anything. But I can't believe so many people are here." I look around at the crowd in the private dining room. "There are friends from high school, college, medical school, and even my residency."

"I talked to a guy named Jim who went through residency with you. He's quite the fan."

I can't be sure if he's stating a fact or if he's jealous. "I wouldn't have made it through school without him. He was a rock. Did you meet his wife? I'm sure I saw her in this sea of people."

"I didn't meet her, but he mentioned her. I also met your college roommate, Elaine Gray. I didn't realize you knew her. She's running for US Senate."

"I'm going to vote for her. And not because I've held her hair more than once while she threw up in a toilet, but because she would be a great senator."

A big smile covers his face, and he's so handsome that my heart skips a beat. "Actually, I donated to her campaign a few weeks ago. I have to admit, I'm a little star struck by her."

His politics match mine, and that only makes me fall harder for him. "That makes sense. She's remarkable."

He leans in and whispers in my ear, "I got you a beautiful LaPerla pantie and corset set. I'd understand if you wouldn't want to show me how well it fits since I was such a jerk, but the invitation is open."

Nice of him to admit that now. I'm mad at him, but I can't stay that way, not with those beautiful brown eyes staring back at me. I've fallen so hard for him, and I'm sure we would both agree that the sex is fucking incredible, but I'm thirty-three now and need to consider that if I want a family, good sex just isn't enough.

Cameron has hinted that there may not be a family in his future, though I'm not sure if it's by choice or by circumstance. However, it's hard to say no to the idea of a naughty birthday night.

"I might like that, but I wonder if we need to have that conversation you've been hinting at first. Without a doubt, we do the horizontal mamba well together, but there's something you've been suggesting you want to discuss, and I may want something that I'm not sure you want. We probably need to figure that out together first."

He pauses, and his eyes flicker when he registers what I'm saying. "I see."

Before he can continue, Dillon walks up with Emerson. "Birthday girl!"

"I have the shock on your face on video. You were completely surprised," Emerson says.

"I had no clue what you guys were planning. This came out of left field for sure."

Apparently, with the RSVP card, each person specified a meal choice, so we're soon ushered to our sit-down dinner. I wander from table to table, enjoying being the center of all this attention. Better than half of the guests have found rooms here in Napa, and the other half will head home.

I'm thrilled when I spot Andy and realize he supplied the wine. "Andy! What a wonderful surprise."

"I'm honored to be invited."

"I'm hoping CeCe gave you more than twenty-four hours' notice."

"She did. She ordered the wine from me quite some time ago and encouraged me to join you."

"What a treat for everyone. Have you seen Greer?"

"Oh yes. We had a wonderful chat about wine." Changing subjects, he asks, "Do you really know all these people?"

I gaze around the room as I take a seat in the empty chair next to him. "There are so many of my friends from so many parts of my life." Pointing across the room, I ask, "Do you see that woman in the bright pink dress?"

"Of course."

"Her name's Michele. She went to elementary school with CeCe and me. Her father was president of some bank, and they moved to New York City when we were maybe ten years old. We've always kept in touch, and she's now married and living in Minneapolis with an executive from a big box store." Looking around, I spot another friend. "See the gentleman over there? That's Michael, my date to prom my junior year. When we were in school, he was a football player with dark curly locks of hair. Now look at him."

"Ah, the bald man with a potbelly. I met him earlier. He's funny and has a cute wife, and together they have five kids. He wants to sell me some life insurance later."

"Oh no. I'm so sorry."

"I'll manage. Who's the man Greer is talking to?"

"That's Sebastian. We went to medical school together. I believe he's a thoracic surgeon in Palo Alto."

"Doctor, huh?"

"And his husband is over at the bar picking up drinks for the three of them."

Andy appears relieved. "You have many friends, but you don't have a boyfriend, right?"

"I've always felt very lucky with so many friends, but no, I currently don't have a boyfriend." I launch into the story of my house burning down and living in a friend's downstairs apartment.

Andy shares stories of his friends and growing up in Argentina and Italy. The DJ interrupts him when he starts calling for me. "Where's our birthday girl, Hadlee?"

I politely excuse myself as CeCe takes the mike and asks

everyone to lift their glass in a toast. "To my oldest, dearest, and my sister by choice. You deserve only the best. May this new year make your every dream come true. Happy birthday, Hadlee."

"Happy birthday" is repeated by most in the room, and we're all stunned as the staff rolls out a glorious cake with fresh white rose decorations and a pale yellow frosting. The cake is adorned with a sparkler which burns out as everyone sings the birthday song.

CeCe hands me the microphone, and a voice that I believe is Dillon calls out, "What did you wish?"

I gaze across the room at Cameron. Our eyes lock, and I smile. He beams at me, and I say, "I'll never tell. It may not come true."

I turn to CeCe and grab her hand. "Thank you to CeCe, Emerson, and Greer for planning such a wonderful surprise. I really had no idea. I love you guys." The room applauds the girls, and I wait for the ovation to stop. "It's so wonderful to see all of you from so many parts of my life. You all have made such wonderful impacts on me, making me who I am today, and I'll never be able to thank you enough for showing me how lucky I am. Many of you know that twenty-four years ago today, my mother died of breast cancer, which often makes my birthday difficult to celebrate. Thank you all for helping me today. I love you all."

The room stands and applauds, which only makes me tear up as CeCe, Emerson, and Greer all stand to hug me.

CeCe announces, "Because of all of you tonight, we'll donate over $100,000 to women's breast cancer research. Thank you for your generosity. Make sure to try the cake. I promise it's amazing."

I'm stunned and moved all at the same time. I can't stop the tears from falling down my face. They're not only tears of sadness for the loss of my mother, or joy because so many people seem to care about me, but also because I'm so moved by everyone's kindness on a topic so important to me.

The staff has been busy passing pieces of raspberry filling between the delicate layers of lemon cake. Even the crazy rainbow mosaic of flakes sprinkled across the top add to the celebration. I take a bite and it practically melts in my mouth; the light perfection of the cake itself and the richness of the cream cheese frosting has the calling card of elegance.

As the evening winds to a close, cake crumbs and smears of frosting are all that remain of the once triple layered cake. With the dessert finished, the chatter in the room rises and falls, and wineglasses are filled and emptied until all too soon, it's time for the guests to make their way home or to their hotels.

CeCe has made arrangements for the gifts to be moved to our chalet. The money collected for breast cancer research means so much to me. It warms my heart that my friends are so generous. I know just the agency to donate this to under my mom's name.

I search for Cameron, but I don't find him. I was hoping to finish our conversation and maybe enjoy some time together, though he probably thinks I'm a psycho after our conversation got interrupted. He makes my heart beat faster, my stomach turn, and my knees weak while at the same time. He's smart, funny, and if I'm honest, he's incredible in bed.

I want more than sex with him, and while he may feel that he isn't capable of more, but I know he is.

chapter
TWENTY-THREE

CAMERON

It's only Monday afternoon, but it feels like a Thursday. I have too many things going on. I feel like the old circus act where the performer spins multiple plates on a stick, and he keeps adding more as the rotation of the others continues. I feel like all the plates I'm spinning are about to fall.

My phone buzzes. "Yes?"

"Cameron, there's a doctor on the phone for you. He says it's an emergency."

When I pick up the phone, it's my father's doctor, who's called to tell me that my dad collapsed in his exam room and they're admitting him to University Hospital. I ask a few clarifying questions, but because of certain rules he doesn't tell me much, so I'm left to determine if I really need to go to the hospital. After thinking about it a few moments, I realize I'm foolish to debate this. I need to be with my father.

Calling a Lyft, I tell my admin, "Jeannine, my dad's been admitted to University Hospital. I need to go. I have my computer and my cell phone if anyone needs me."

"Of course. Is there anything I can do?"

"If you could let Mason and Dillon know, but I don't know anything else right now. I'll keep you posted if I need anything," I say over my shoulder as I walk toward the elevators.

When I arrive, the information desk directs me to his fourth-floor room. My father's dressed in a hospital gown, a look of shock on his pale face. "Cameron? What are you doing here?"

"Your doctor called and said you collapsed in his office. You didn't tell me you were here seeing a doctor. What happened?"

"It's nothing really."

"Dad, people don't drive three hours to see a doctor in San Francisco even if they have a son in the city. And they don't collapse unless there's a problem."

He gets angry with me and stubbornly says, "It ain't nothin'."

His hands are frail and shaking slightly as he reaches for the water cup on the table over his bed. His movements are so much of the man he was and still is. They're ashen where the sunlight catches them, though not ghostly, just subdued and a yellow-gray. I think this is the first time I realize how vulnerable he is and how much of a toll the sickness is taking. A sickness I was too self-absorbed to notice.

He dozes during some replay of an eighties football game on the small television in his room. I take a seat next to him and open my computer. He doesn't want to talk or tell me what's going on, so I'll stay with him and work. I slog my way through several hundred lines of code, hoping to find the mistake and figure out if I can fix it, but I've only managed to read the same line at least a dozen times. I'm not concentrating, and nothing about it sticks in my memory.

The doctor comes in. "Mr. Newhouse?"

I stand and extend my hand. "Hello, Doctor. How's my dad doing?"

"What do you know about his condition?"

My dad's now fully awake and pretending to be engrossed in the football game. "Not very much, I'm afraid. He's been rather protective of what's going on with his health."

"I see." Turning to my dad, the doctor asks, "Michael, how are you feeling?"

He stares at me nervously, and his hands are shaking from what I assume is the DTs. "Not too good, Doc."

"Okay, I'll have the nurse give you another dose of benzodiazepine. Excuse me. I'll return in a minute."

I watch my dad. "Are you sure there isn't anything I should know?"

The doctor returns with a nurse on his heels before he can answer, injecting a large syringe into his IV. My dad quickly and visibly relaxes, and the tremors almost stop.

I glance at the doctor. "He won't tell me what's going on."

He stares at his charts and says, "Are you aware that he's given you his medical power of attorney?"

I sigh. "No."

"Let's step outside." He points to the door, and I follow him out. "Mr. Newhouse, your dad's quite ill. His cirrhosis is at an advanced stage, and while his liver is beginning to shut down, he seems to have also developed a few cancerous tumors in his lungs."

I'm surprised and not sure what to say. *Cirrhosis and cancer? Does this mean he's going to die? Wait!* I blink and stare at the doctor in horror. My hands tremble as I try to understand exactly what he's telling me. My heart races wildly, and I'm breathless. I do not understand a word of the doctor's careful explanation of my dad's condition. "How can that be possible?" The question screams on repeat in my head. A thousand questions for my dad run through my mind, but all I can think to ask the doctor is "Can we do radiation and chemotherapy?"

"We're starting a new round tomorrow. He needs to finish the withdrawals from some of the medication he's been on. We're trying to be aware of his sobriety."

My legs are weak, and I need to sit down. Finding a chair, I sink into it. Running through my mind are all the terrible things I've done and said to my dad. I put my face in my hands, trying to hold off on the tears as I whisper, "I see. Is it terminal?"

"He has a lot going on. The cirrhosis is in an advanced stage, and a replacement is difficult. He's been sober for several years, which allows him to be on the list, but there are many other factors involved, most of which come from availability."

Without even thinking, I ask, "Can I give him part of my liver?" My heart beats faster from the hope.

"I suggested that a few months ago, and he was pretty adamant that you weren't interested."

"Doctor, my father and I have been estranged for a while. I didn't realize my dad was coming to San Francisco until he showed up at my office earlier this week. And I didn't understand he was seeing a doctor until you called to tell me that he collapsed in your exam room earlier today. We do have a troubled relationship on many levels, but if my liver's compatible, I'll give him part of it without hesitation."

"We'll have to do some tests, but let's see how he's going to respond to the chemo and radiation. If we can shrink the tumors small enough in his lungs that we can operate, we can discuss the transplant."

The doctor leaves, and I call Dillon and Mason to tell them the news. They put me on speakerphone so I can talk to them jointly.

"Wow, man, I'm so sorry," Dillon empathizes.

"Take however much time you need," Mason shares.

"Thanks. I'll keep you posted, but for now I'm working, just from the hospital."

"What do you need from your house?" Mason asks.

"I'll call Hadlee and see if she can bring a few things over. I've got it covered."

"Well, let me know if I can bring anything from the office, or if you need anything at all, okay?"

"Promise. Thanks, guys."

I hang up, then debate what I want to say to Hadlee. She's a doctor, so she must have experience in this area. I call her next.

As the phone rings in my ear, I'm still working on what I need. It goes to her voice mail, and she singsongs in her message. "Hello, this is Hadlee. I can't take your call right now. You know what to do." *Beep.*

"Hadlee, it's me, Cameron. I'm at University Hospital with my dad. Can you stop by my place and bring me a few changes of clothes? I may be here a while. I'd appreciate it."

A FEW HOURS LATER, after grabbing a sandwich and Diet Coke from the hospital cafeteria, I enter the room to find Hadlee talking to my dad, his chart in her hands.

"What are you doing?" I demand.

"I'm checking out his chart." She points to a bag in a chair. "I brought you some clothes. I can tell you where you can get a shower here in the hospital."

I want her to leave. I need to figure this out with my dad, just us. "Thanks, but I'm good." I don't want everyone to know what's going on with him. We don't need their pity, damn it.

"Would you like me to explain some of the things they're doing with your dad? I'm happy to translate some of the medical jargon if you'd like."

"No. Thanks for bringing my clothes. You can leave now." This is a private matter. I don't need my friends trying to make me feel better. My dad needs me, and I need to concentrate on him. No distractions.

She's visibly stunned by my directness. "Cameron, how can you be so cold? I'm only trying to help." She keeps her eyes steady, but I can tell there's sorrow already building.

"He's my father, Hadlee. I already told you not to put yourself in the middle of this."

Rather than leave, she stays rooted to the spot, the breeze from an open window moving her hair away from the cheekbones that have become so much more prominent over the previous weeks. Her features buckle slightly before she speaks, the only betrayal of her anguish. "There was a time when you enjoyed spending time with me, remember? Yet you give me up as soon as there's a threat to the balance in your life. That isn't how you treat your friends, or at least not a version I can respect. You've broken me, and now you're attacking the pieces. There isn't a woman alive who wants a man who would betray her like you're doing. But don't worry, I'll leave you to your life. We have friends in common, but we never have to interact again."

Hadlee's face is paler than I've ever recalled it being, as if her very blood was shrinking away from my presence, her lips almost ghostly despite the light of the room.

I'm shocked by her tirade. I can't explain to her that this is too much at one time, but I deserve everything she's said. I know I'm being an ass when I concentrate on the view outside the window and a passing plane instead of apologizing, but I'm mad. More at myself than her, but rather than tell her as much, I snap, "You don't realize how it was. You like to judge me, but have you any idea what I did for you? Any idea at all?" Then I turn my back to her, face set like an adversary, eyes cold, muscles tense.

There's disappointment in my father's eyes. Maybe now she'll understand the anger I work so hard to hide and why I don't deserve anyone's love.

She seems quiet, angry, and sad all within a sixty-second window.

My father yells, "Cameron! I didn't raise you to behave like this."

My anger spews like a volcano. "Of course not. You didn't raise me at all."

"I'm going to miss you," she whispers, eyes beginning to fill with unshed tears.

"Cameron, I think you need to leave and go cool down," my dad pleads.

"Don't worry about it, Michael," Hadlee tells him. Watching

me carefully, so she knows she's being heard, she says, "Cameron's just worried about you. I need to return to my rounds. I'll let you two continue your afternoon." She turns and almost runs out the door.

My dad turns to glare at me. "I know I made a lot of mistakes with you after your mother died, but that was completely uncalled for. You need to go after her and apologize."

"Mind your own business."

"You *are* my business. She's a sweet girl, and she deserves better than you, but somehow she likes you. So pull your head out of your ass and go after her."

Rather than do what he says, I sit in my chair and eat my sandwich.

Fuck her. Now she understands what I've been telling her.

I'm not the guy for her.

chapter
TWENTY-FOUR

HADLEE

I'M HEARTBROKEN THAT CAMERON was such a jerk, but it's a giant neon sign that he was only interested in sex and nothing more. And now he isn't even interested in sex.

I wasn't trying to get in the middle of anything; I only wanted to share my expertise and hopefully make it a bit less stressful for them. I like Michael, and I was falling for Cameron. I understand that they have a challenging relationship, but that's for them to figure out. My only hope was to help explain what seems like an intimidating situation and make it less scary, but so much for that.

I can't live in his house anymore. He hasn't called to apologize for the episode at the hospital last week. Ever since our blowup, I've essentially been avoiding him. He has my number and hasn't called or texted me. I've waited long enough; now it's time to move on. Each evening, I come home and hide in my room, doing my charts and returning e-mails from my bed. I believe he owes me an apology, and he hasn't reached out to me at all. *Fuck him!*

I thought we made a good team. Ever since Cameron helped by calling my insurance company with me, they agreed to cover the reconstruction process. What a relief it was to know I'll get my home back again. And with CeCe's help, we're getting closer to being done.

I have water and electricity, and while it isn't perfect, I've decided I'm going to move home. Cameron's angry with me for inserting myself, and he obviously doesn't want what I want. I've already fallen for him, but it's smarter to just rip the Band-Aid off before I really go head over heels for him.

I'm so grateful he gave me a place to stay and at no cost, but it's time to give him his privacy back. He's a good friend, and maybe after I get over the rejection, we can be friends again. His generosity came at the right time. I needed the reprieve because the insurance deductible's off-the-charts expensive and I don't have much savings, plus my debt from medical school. I miss my house and my things. Granted, not much was able to be salvaged throughout the house, but I've found several good substitutes if I couldn't find the real thing, and thanks to my bedroom door being shut, most of my personal belongings were saved, including a picture of my mom and dad when I was eight years old.

I never aspired to a large home, preferring cozy and friendly. It's the perfect space for my needs and many of my wants. It's my "cottage" in the city, furnished with everything rustic, the old being a stage for my new creations, new paintings daubed on perfect squares of canvas. Space is just space until you bring your own personality to it, make your mark, express what's sacred to you.

I need to tell Cameron I'm moving out. I think I should tell him in person, but I can't bring myself to do it. I guess we're both avoiding each other, when I really think about it. I know he has a lot going on between his work and his dad's illness, so I don't push. Finally, I decide to just text him.

Me: Hey. I really want to thank you for allowing me to stay in your rental. My place has electricity and water and is almost ready, so I'll be moving out this weekend. I've made arrangements with your housekeeper to come in on Monday to clean at my expense, and I'll place the key in an envelope and drop it in your mail slot. Thank you again. Please let me know if there's anything I can do for you.

He doesn't respond, and it makes me depressed. I hid from him, but if I'm honest with myself, I wanted him to apologize. I understand his dad's in a bad place, but I did him a favor by picking his things up, and he responds by yelling at me.

I'm on the patio in the candlelight, enjoying the backyard one last time when I notice the lights come on upstairs. I'm trying to destress by just concentrating on all the things I have to do when I hear him slide open the upstairs door, the light jazz coming from my unit probably alerting him to my presence. I'm sure I can feel his eyes on me, but I won't glance at him to be sure.

"Hey."

I turn to see him halfway down the stairs. "Hey. Did you get my text?"

I can see him in the muted light of the setting sun. He looks tired, but he still makes my heart race, my stomach clench, and my panties wet. "I did. I haven't been a very good friend. You don't have to leave if your place isn't done yet."

I can't change my mind. It's time to get some distance. "I

know, but I figure I can get out of your way now so you can get it rented and actually make some money."

He takes his baseball cap off and runs his hands through his hair. "I'm not hurting for money. Please stay as long as you need. I'm not going to rent it for a while. And my housekeeper will clean the place. You don't have to pay her for that."

I can't give in. I see the desperation in his eyes, but I must be strong. "I don't mind. It's the least I can do."

He reaches for my hand. "I'm sorry I'm such a shitty friend."

I carefully pull my hand away and put it in my lap, pinching the soft spot between my thumb and forefinger, hoping the pain will distract me enough that I don't cry. "We want different things."

He sits back and looks surprised. "We do? What do you want that's different from what I want?"

We've never talked about it, but it's time to be honest with him. "I want to get married and have kids."

He can't look me in the eye. "You do?" Cameron sighs loudly. "I'm not good at relationships. My parents were terrible examples, and I'm pretty screwed up. You've seen it. I'm not marriage material."

I scrutinize him carefully. "Cameron, I'm not sure anyone's good at relationships. They take work, and you have to be willing to do that work. My home life growing up wasn't perfect by any means, but I want to do better for my kids one day." I wait for a response, but he doesn't even glance at me. Gathering my things from the table, I say, "I better get to bed. Good night, Cameron. I'll see you... I guess when I see you."

He doesn't call after me or follow me, and it makes me cry

big ugly tears as I lie in bed, thinking about Cameron and the last few months. I'm not working tomorrow, so I'll meet the movers at my storage unit in the late morning. I hate to leave the comfort of his home and the connection here, but I can't take the rift between us anymore and feels it's for the best. We want different things.

I replay our conversation over and over. I could've taken it in so many different directions. He stared at me like a stranger, yet worse. Instead of the fragile soul he's had the opportunity to know, he sees an adversary in me, even though I never sought to upset him or insert myself into his situation. It's as if he hates me. Okay, hate may be too strong a word, but from what I saw with my parents and have seen over the years, it takes a strong hate to break a strong love, to erect walls, to protect the self.

That can't be us though. It can't be the end of our story. Can we find a fragment of at least a friendship we can share? A seed that might grow into a new relationship—a friendship to heal us both?

I believe in him and seem to give him more credit than he gives himself. I understand him, and I wish he could see the person he is to me. I know he's been hurt and I'm sorry, truly, yet there has to be a part of him that knows I've also been hurt. If he can be softer, I can be too. I can take down some of those walls a brick at a time.

I let him in and let him see my naked heart. I guess that's best the way to find out who we truly are. Was it all worth it? I'll be wiser from the mess he made, at least.

Thanks, Cameron, for breaking my heart and showing me who you really are. Because of my father, I'll always be a survivor.

chapter TWENTY-FIVE

CAMERON

I WAS SHOCKED when Hadlee's text came this afternoon. I've been debating on how to apologize for being such an asshole. My dad has barely spoken to me since, and now he's refusing my help. He'd rather die than take part of my liver.

I'm such a giant ass.

She was only trying to help, but I couldn't figure out how to apologize, and now she's leaving. I would love to blame it on my dad and all the shit he brings with him, but I need to own this. I barked at her, and she didn't deserve it.

Fuck!

When she told me tonight that she wants to get married and have kids, that threw me for a loop, although I'm not sure why. She's a pediatrician, for God's sake—of course she likes kids, and she probably wants a bunch. The sex is pretty much the best I've ever had, and it kills me that I won't see her every day once she moves back home.

I sit back in my chair and listen to the sounds of the city permeating the dark backyard. All I can think about is her beautiful smile and how I love that I can still smell her after we've spent the day together.

Sitting for some time, I watch the light from the bathroom in her apartment cast shadows on the yard and then grow dark, followed by various lights going on and off. She's definitely going to bed. I wish I knew what I could do to talk her into staying.

Her apartment goes dark and I don't see any more movement. Figuring she's gone to bed, I head upstairs to my place. I'm too upset with myself to sleep though, and all I can think to do is sit in my home office and work.

Turning on my computer and dialing into our company VPN, I scroll through the various technology gossip sites, stopping when a story on one of the start-ups we presented to catches my eye. They threw us under the bus by sharing all of our confidential information a few months ago, including Dillon's financial evaluations.

In the blurb, they announce the CEO and CFO have both been fired. *Hmm... I wonder what happened there.* I forward the article to Mason, Dillon, Emerson, Greer, and Sara, saying, Did you see this? Big changes at Fractional. Very interesting.

I get a quick response from Dillon.

Mason's quick to add, They seemed to have a pretty solid management team if I remember correctly. Emerson?

Yes, it was a good team. Solid experience and excellent firsthand knowledge.

Sara joins the conversation. Trey forwarded the link to his dad. Our lawyers threatened to sue over them sharing Dillon's models and our confidential information, but we couldn't prove anything. It didn't go anywhere. Hopefully Charles can find something out.

We banter back and forth, speculating why they would've suddenly been fired. Sara then adds, Do a quick search of the other companies we recently lost to PK. Does anyone notice the same trend?

I search Smithright Software, Adaptive Technologies, and Flintridge Solutions. Just like Fractional Technologies, they've seen some great changes in their leadership. Holy crap! There's a pattern. Each one has lost at least one of their founders, and it's been pretty discreet. Do we know what's going on?

Dillon inquires, Has anyone heard from Terry Klein? Any word on how he's feeling?

I have a quick inner debate on sharing, mostly because it'll upset Mason the most. I saw him last weekend in the rehab clinic in Foster City. He's doing okay, but they won't release him because he lives alone.

Emerson chides, Can't he afford a full-time nurse?

I'm not sure. PK's struggling, Mason writes.

That's what I needed to hear, Dillon celebrates.

Suddenly there's an e-mail from Greer in the conversation. Sorry, guys. I've been watching your conversation but following up with some friends to find out what seems to be going on. Apparently Perkins Klein has been selling their investments to Benchmark to counter some of their bad investments and remain solvent, and Benchmark has been demanding the changes.

Holy shit! This is what we wanted when we pushed the duds their way, I remind everyone.

I thought we had Quinn sharing what was going on from

the inside. Why didn't we realize this? Mason asks.

Good question. Who's fleecing Perkins Klein's investments? Emerson asks.

I think we need to make this the top of the agenda on Sunday night, Sara responds.

Agreed, I return.

We all sign off and go about our evenings. I stare at my computer and the over three hundred e-mails that came in today that I haven't even looked at. One by one, I slowly go through them, the work distracting me from my personal life. When I finally check the clock, it's after 3:00 a.m.

I shut my computer off and head to the bedroom, leaving a trail of clothes behind me as I fall into bed and dream about Hadlee.

chapter TWENTY-SIX

HADLEE

I've only lived here for six months. How did I accumulate so much crap? I wipe the sweat from my brow as a knock sounds at my front door. *Who could that be?*

I stare through the peephole, then open the door to Cameron. "Hello." I step back so he can come in. "What has you home this morning?"

He hands me a cup of coffee. "I ended up working until after three, so I've been slow to get going today."

Grateful for the coffee, I take a big whiff and admit, "I really needed this. Thanks. I'm sorry if I woke you this morning."

"You didn't. I just wanted to see you."

He was avoiding me, and now he wants to see me? The twinkle in his eyes and the way his T-shirt stretches across his chest make my insides all gooey, and I can't help but flirt with him. "Well, I'm not very cute this morning with all this." I wave to my sweat-covered, makeup-free face and what I'm sure are wet circles under my arms.

"You're beautiful." Softening his tone, he continues, "You're always beautiful."

I'm taken aback by his comment and my stomach flips. "Err—"

"I owe you a huge apology for biting your head off about my dad. I understand you were only trying to help. He and I have such a difficult relationship that I don't have a lot of patience when it comes to him."

Staring at my sneakers, I mutter, "I shouldn't have inserted myself into the situation. I like you both, and I only wanted to share my expertise."

He steps forward and brushes a wisp of hair away from my face, then cups my cheek. "Please don't leave," he whispers.

I shut my eyes and take in what he's saying. It's what I've wanted to hear from him, but only part of it. "Cameron, I can't live here indefinitely."

"Yes, you can." He bends over, and our lips meet softly for a short moment. Then his kiss becomes aggressive, his tongue pushing between my lips and tasting of his morning coffee. He takes my mouth as if it belongs to him. A groan tickles in my throat, wanting to give him everything he wants. I'm confused, both happy and unsure, but I can't stop. My entire body throbs to feel every inch of him, my legs weak.

He pushes me against the wall, pulling my T-shirt over my head and unclasping my bra in one swift movement. "You have the most beautiful breasts," he murmurs, then buries himself in my heaving cleavage while playing with both nipples.

I should tell him to stop, but I can't. I need this.

"I'm getting hard thinking about my handprint on your bare ass as your pussy's helplessly spread wide open while you're tied to the headboard."

My heart beats faster as I drop to my knees and start undoing his jeans.

"Fuck me, you're enchanting." He tangles his fingers in my hair as I bring the tip of his cock to my lips. I pull his body closer to me and take him completely into my mouth. His whole body shudders, and I groan as I suck deeper until I feel his cock at the back of my throat. I back away, then slide him into me once more.

I set the rhythm, backing away to the tip and then descending upon him, taking him almost to the point of gagging. This may be a mistake, but I want it, and I need him. No one has ever made me feel like he does.

He groans and starts to join my rhythm, one hand on the back of my head, the other clenching the side of the counter. His fingers pull and push on my scalp, encouraging me as he moans his appreciation.

His hips tremble slightly as I cup his balls. They're tight, swollen, and I massage them tenderly as I pump him in and out of my mouth.

This is everything.

"I'm going to come," he growls.

And he does. I keep my mouth on him as he spasms, the salty sweet liquid bursting into my mouth. I swallow all of it hungrily.

It's my turn now as he moves me from inside the door into the bedroom of the suite. He lays me on my back and gets comfortable between my legs. I watch him in the mirrored closet doors. God, he's beautiful. He rubs his finger up my slit, and I moan.

He inserts his fingers into my slick channel, massaging that sweet spot deep inside. He licks me from bottom to top and continues to work my clit. "My God, you're an extraordinary creature," he whispers.

I lick my lips nervously and close my eyes. My breasts are displayed before him like a buffet. My nipples are pebbled and hard, and my mouth waters at the thought of another taste of his cock.

I gasp as he thoroughly licks my pussy. He's prolonging it, not to torture me but to make my orgasm more intense. I can't take it anymore, and I push into his face. He goes deep inside me, eating me harder and faster, sucking my clit and open-mouthed kissing my tight pussy, the pussy that was made for him. The dam breaks as I moan my pleasure and involuntarily scream his name.

I can't seem to catch my breath, and I'm completely satisfied.

He stares deep into my eyes. "Ready for some fun?"

I nod as he removes a foil package from his pocket and sheathes his hard and anxious cock. Licking my lips seems to make him grow even harder. He turns me over and positions my ass high in the air. In the mirror, it's erotic to watch him rub his finger along my slit, his hands digging into my hips, fingertips bruising. That's the only warning he gives before slamming into me so hard that I let out a shriek of pain and surprise. He withdraws and then pushes in again, an animal concerned only with a primal mating drive. He owns me in the purest sense as he slams into me again and again, a blunt force trauma that my body accepts in pure sexual shock. The teasing from before and the pain right now all blend together in a whirlwind of sensation.

He slams his hand hard on my ass and my pussy clamps, the pain and pleasure intermingling. "Harder," I whisper, though

I'm not sure who I'm saying it for—him or me. I'm not sure it matters; we're the same being when he's inside me, moving toward one goal.

He pulls back, gathering my hair in his hand. There's a brief moment of respite, a cold reminder of the space he's claimed. Then he's fully inside me, pulling me by the hair so his cock is as deep as it can possibly be. His invasion is thorough, his cock pulsing in cruel pleasure.

My body convulses, on the verge of another orgasm, on the edge of passing out, torn between pleasure and pain. I release what I believe is a pent-up sound of grief, though I'm not entirely sure. I'm in a state of pure bliss as I shatter, my orgasm coming suddenly, making my insides bear down, my hips buck against him. He shouts behind me, his cock pulsing fresh heat into my sex. He draws out his orgasm and mine, pushing his still-firm cock into my slick channel with lazy thrusts, every slide a new wave of sparks behind my eyes.

"I'm imagining your sexy body bound in restraints, writhing in desperation, screaming out my name for a release you've yet to comprehend."

A twinge of lust and excitement overtakes me. I like that idea, and it makes me want him more.

"You're so goddam beautiful when you come," he whispers in an awestruck tone.

I'm embarrassed by his admission, not sure that I ever want to see that look on my face. "I'm going to need to get going to meet the movers over at my storage unit."

He seems surprised, and his eyes cloud over. "You're still moving out?"

"Cameron, I can't live here forever. My place is livable, and it's time I move home."

"But I thought you wanted to stay."

Sitting up, I say softly, "Cameron, I want more from you than casual sex."

He appears anguished and hurt. "I'm not made for relationships. This is all I'm able to give. Can't this be enough?"

That only further confirms that I'm making the right decision. If I stay, all it's going to be is good sex. While that's nice in the short term, when I realize I'm too old to have kids and have wasted too many years on him, I'll regret this and hate him. If I get out now, maybe I can salvage a friendship, or we can at least be civil when we see each other at our common friends' events.

Part of me wants so much to stay, but the smart part of me is telling me to rip the Band-Aid off now; the longer it stays on, the harder it'll be to remove.

"I'm sorry, but no. I don't think you give yourself enough credit. I want it all, and I'd love it with you, but only if you want it, too."

I stand and begin to dress as he removes the used condom and walks to the bathroom. I hear the toilet flush and the water run in the sink. He doesn't say anything, and I think that's more hurtful than if he yelled and told me why he wants me to stay.

When he returns to the bedroom with his clothes in hand and begins to dress, I walk to the bathroom to clean up. I hear my front door open and shut and realize he's gone.

I stare at myself in the bathroom mirror. My mascara's smeared under my tear-filled eyes.

I want more than great sex, and damn it, I deserve more.

chapter
TWENTY-SEVEN

CAMERON

I CAN'T HELP BUT BE ANGRY that she's making these demands on me. Why can't we ease into this? She can live downstairs, and we could spend most nights together and enjoy lots of naughty sex. *Fuck, why is this so hard!*

I hear her leave to meet her moving van, the pit in my stomach that started when I was an ass at the hospital having grown tremendously. I'm disappointed that she won't be here when I get back.

I think of this morning as I lie upon the soft feather mattress, cocooning myself in the silk sheets as I imagine Hadlee standing at the bottom of the bed. I gaze upon her perfect naked form, her skin glistening with a sensual sweat. My eye's drawn to the auburn river that gently caresses its way along her neck, reaching just below her shoulder blades. *If the gods are real, then this woman's their masterpiece.* I love the way her blue eyes light up when she sees me. Her smile that makes my heart beat seconds faster. She thinks I'm a better man than I know I am, and that both excites and depresses me.

With a sigh, I get up and dressed before climbing on my bike and starting it up. The roar of the engine helps me to forget about Hadlee, at least for a few minutes.

When I arrive at the office, there's a noticeable buzz for a Saturday. I bump into Greer as I walk into the kitchen. "That was quite the bombshell last night," I mutter.

"I know! I have more feelers out and will be interested to hear what we learn today. I think Charles is hoping for a meeting with the partners tonight."

"I can make that work."

When I return to my office, I take a seat and stare at the software that was sent over to us for a new app designed for expense tracking. It's nothing new, and I think back to the sex Hadlee and I had earlier. My cock stirs in my pants. I have to come up with a way to get her to change her mind.

My text alert pings.

Greer: Charles 8 p.m.

At least that'll distract me from the fact that my house will be silent and dark tonight when I get home, and she'll be gone.

Me: I'll be there.

Before I realize it, Dillon and Emerson are at my door. "Do you want a ride to Charles's?"

Checking the time on my cell phone, I see it's already after seven. *How did that happen?* "Oh, yeah. That'd be great. Do you mind?"

"Not at all," Emerson assures me.

Sara, Greer, and Mason join us as we pile into Dillon's SUV and start working our way to Hillsboro. Most of the stop-and-go traffic has dissipated, but it's still thick. During the lull, I keep thinking about Hadlee.

"Don't you agree, Cameron?" Sara asks, interrupting my daydream.

"I'm sorry, what?"

"Can you believe Hadlee can move back into her place already?"

"It seems rather quick. She could've stayed longer. I wasn't in any hurry for her to leave." Emerson and Dillon exchange a look. "Someone needs to check on her. She mentioned that she had water and electricity, but that doesn't mean it's ready for moving in."

"I think someone has a crush on Hadlee," Greer singsongs.

I bristle at the notion. "I'll admit to caring that she's safe, but I didn't kick her out. She could live in my apartment for years, and I'd be fine with that." I add in a murmur, "More than fine."

Emerson reaches back and pats my leg. "Cam, we love you, and we know Hadlee's crazy about you. We support you both."

I wish they understand that supporting us means they need to be as worried as I am about her living situation. This is a big deal. Her place isn't ready to be moved into, I just know it.

As we pull into the Spanish-style home and the pack of dogs comes rushing to greet us, I'm glad to no longer be the topic of conversation. CeCe pulls up right behind us with Trey in the car. Sara immediately goes over to him, and they have a long and lingering kiss.

Why is it we all have to couple up? First, it was Dillon and Emerson, and then it was Trey and Sara. Plus Mason's seeing Annabel. I miss when it was only us without the complications of significant others.

As we gather in Charles's office, Jim, the private investigator, joins us. "Dillon, you mentioned you found something today?"

"Yes. It seems our mole's not discriminatory. I think they've been selling our research to a few others in The Valley."

"What makes you think that?" Charles asks.

Dillon passes a packet of paper around to each of us. "Check out these spreadsheets I've compiled. We always track who wins, and while the majority of them have gone to Perkins Klein, we've also found that Benchmark, Argent Capital, and Carson Mills each have won a few that are surprising. Plus they're picking up the pieces Perkins Klein is selling off, none of which are being offered to us."

"How can we be sure this is the mole and not investments made by our competitors?" Greer asks.

"Because these are the numbers we put into our research that was fed to the mole."

Mason glances up from his spreadsheets. "Who could the leak be?"

My blood boils. "This affects our bottom line, and it pisses me off. Who the fuck did we upset?"

Jim answers glibly, "Anyone you didn't fund, or someone who can't afford that Fat Boy with all the upgrades you ride."

I roll my eyes. As if my Harley was an actual reason that someone would go this hard at us.

Emerson, always the peacekeeper, interjects, "We've pissed someone off. But we're seeing less loss, aren't we?"

Mason and Charles both agree.

"So what should we do next?" Greer asks. "I'd love to do a hardcore public relations piece on us in the *New York Times.* I think I have someone who would write it for us."

Mason and I stare at one another. "That would work," I tell her.

"I think it's time I start shopping my new start-up and see how the funding shakes out," Charles suggest. He outlines his prospective company to us, and we listen with rapt attention. Greer's typing notes on her computer, and we devise our plan on how we'll take on this new challenge we're facing.

IT'S AFTER ELEVEN when Emerson and Dillon drop me off at my dark condo. I consider calling Hadlee, but I don't. Instead, I write a text message to her, asking how the day went, but never send it. In my heart of hearts, I know it would only be a booty call.

I lie in bed, and I think of her. Hadlee could grace any billboard or magazine cover, but she was better than those two-dimensional photoshopped models. Somehow her imperfections make her perfect. There's a shyness to her, a hesitation in her body movements and a softness in her voice.

I picture her in jeans and a T-shirt, feet up on the couch and painting her nails. She's right there, only feet away, but in her understated glamour, she might as well be on the television or a girl in a music video.

She left. She moved to her own place. I may never see her again, but that's all right. She didn't need a guy with a lot of emotional baggage like me anyway.

I need to move on and focus on my job. Sleep usually avoids me, but tonight I'm too tired to even walk the fifty steps to my bedroom. I pull a throw from the back of the leather couch and fall into a restless sleep. dreaming of Hadlee.

She lives with me in my dreams.

chapter TWENTY-EIGHT

HADLEE

THE RESTAURANT SPREADS OUT in front of me, dark walnut tables surrounded by maroon leather booths. The large room's arranged in such a way that almost every person's visible from here but no one directly faces us.

I follow the hostess in her black miniskirt as she wobbles on her high heels to a table in the middle of the room. I'm meeting Ken, one of the other doctors working on Lilly's case.

I study the menu. I really want a bacon cheeseburger and fries—they're known for the best in the city—but my clothes are getting a bit snug. As I look over the various salad options, nothing seems appealing to me. Because of the construction, I don't have any kitchen appliances, so all I've done is eat out. I need to be strong and eat some veggies. I learned the contractor's not happy that I'm currently living in my place. He thinks the inspectors won't be okay with it, but they'll never know. I only sleep there, so he'll get over it.

I look up as Ken arrives. "Hadlee," he purrs as he opens his arms for a hug that seems to last a few seconds too long.

Fuck it, cheeseburger it is. I can start my diet again tomorrow. Even if tomorrow never comes.

"You're beautiful tonight, Hadlee."

"Thank you. Of course, you're used to seeing me in jeans and a lab coat."

"You're also beautiful in a lab coat."

Wanting to change the subject, I ask, "How's Lilly holding up?"

"She's fine. Tell me, how are you doing?"

Ken's hand wanders to my leg, and I politely brush it away. I'm not interested in him in the least. "Ken, I'm not really comfortable with your hand on my leg. You live with Vanessa, and I don't mess with men who are involved with other women."

"Vanessa doesn't ever have to know."

I try to look happy because I have to work with him and don't want it to be uncomfortable, but my patience is running thin. "Ken, I thought we were here to talk about Lilly."

He softly rubs my arm, caressing me, and every nerve in my body wants to yell, "Stop."

I push his hand away and firmly state, "If you can't keep this professional, then I'll leave."

In a slick and syrupy voice, he tells me, "Well, you're no fun."

"No, I'm not. Please tell me about Lilly. She's on my schedule later this week, and I'd like to understand what you're suggesting as her oncologist."

"I have no idea. I'll send over her notes."

The waitress arrives as I stand to leave. "Thanks, Ken, for meeting me and wasting my time." I throw my napkin on the table and call a Lyft, having them drop me off at the grocery store so I can hit their salad bar. It isn't perfect, but it's better than a cheeseburger and fries—well, as long as I have some lettuce with the salad dressing.

When I get home, I'm surprised to find Cameron's motorcycle sitting in my driveway, but he's nowhere to be seen. Good thing I didn't drive to the restaurant. I walk into my house and head up the stairs, surprised to hear the television on. "Hello?"

"Hey. Up here. Your contractor let me in as he was leaving."

"That makes me feel safe," I reply sarcastically.

"Have you looked around your place?" He points to the lack of walls in my kitchen, the hanging wires in the living room, and a nail that was missed in the cleanup. "The contractor tells me you have no heat and that if the inspectors catch you here, he'll be fined."

"Cameron, it's only the kitchen. I have water—"

"But no *hot* water, or heat. The contractor was very clear that you aren't supposed to be living here."

"I can shower at the hospital, and that's what blankets and sweaters are for."

"Was living under my roof so bad that you'd put your life in jeopardy and live in these conditions? And workmen are coming and going all the time, too."

I sit in a chair and cover my face. I can't believe I'm going to be this honest. "Cameron, you don't understand. I have feelings for you that aren't reciprocated. You don't want what I want." My voice cracks as I fight back the tears. "I can't live that close to you. Each time we're together, you take a piece of me, and there isn't much of me left."

"Damn it, Hadlee." He takes his baseball cap off and runs his fingers through his hair. Just above a whisper, he argues, "You don't get it at all. I'm totally fucked up. There's something wrong with me. I do have feelings for you, but I don't want you to deal with the mess that is me. You met my dad. You spotted his cirrhosis right away. He was driving the night my mom was killed. That shit messed me up. I have no role models to know how to do relationships well. I'm no prize, and you deserve better than me."

"Why do you get to make the decision for both of us? Plus, are you forgetting my family? My mom dies of breast cancer, and then my dad proceeds to marry seven more times, searching for her replacement. None of the women were interested in his darling daughter, only his checkbook. My history isn't perfect either, but whose is?"

"I don't want you in this house," he begs.

"I have no place to go, and I won't go to your house."

"I'm calling CeCe, then."

"Don't you dare." I stand, ready for a fight. I've gone from hurt to angry in a matter of seconds. "Cameron, you do that and I'll never speak to you again. Just leave."

"Fine. This is a city full of hotels. I'm calling the Marker, and you can stay there. I know the owners."

"What part of this do you not get? I can't afford a hotel at $300 a night." I'm done with this conversation. I plop down in my favorite overstuffed chair. "Just leave, Cameron."

He stares at me, looking puzzled and confused. He doesn't understand why I feel like I do, but that's because he doesn't feel the same about me as I do about him.

"Fine," he says finally, "but this is the last night you can live here. Tomorrow I'm calling CeCe and telling her about your place. And just so you know, I'm sleeping on your couch tonight. You can't be here alone. It isn't safe."

You are not the boss of me. I will never speak to you again if you call CeCe or Greer.

If he calls my friends, that'll be the end of anything. I won't even be able to be friends with him. I'm too upset to talk to him right now; I'll have this conversation with him in the morning when I've had the opportunity to calm down.

I get up and walk into my room, slamming the door shut behind me. That alone helps to calm me down a bit.

Lying in my bed, I look at the ceiling and see some smoke damage. He's probably right. I shouldn't stay here, but I don't have a lot of options right now.

I start to cry.

Damn it, Cameron!

chapter TWENTY-NINE

CAMERON

SHE ABSOLUTELY INFURIATES ME. She can stay for free at my house. And I have no doubt that Greer or CeCe would care if she needed to couch-surf at their place. I want to punch a wall, but not only do I not want to scare her—or me, for that matter—but I don't want to break my hand.

Why can't she see how dangerous it is to stay here?

I'm angry, and I can't sleep. I keep replaying our fight in my head, rationalizing how she needs to move and be far away from me.

I finally fall asleep but am woken with a start when my phone rings. As I answer, I glance at the time on my phone, seeing it's shortly after three. "Hello?"

"Cameron, this is Dr. Morris. I'm sorry for the late call. We may have found a liver donor for your dad. We're going to do surgery in a few hours once the organ arrives. It isn't an easy surgery, and there's the possibility he may not make it. I suggest you come in and visit with your dad before the surgery."

Catching my bearings and trying to see through the fog caused by the lack of sleep, I finally comprehend what he's telling me. "Of course. I'm on my way."

I sit for a minute and process everything he said. *They have a liver coming in. He wasn't a good candidate for a transplant because of the cancer. How the hell did this happen? I can't leave Hadlee here. She can't stay here anymore. It's dangerous.*

Fuck!

I knock on her bedroom door. "Hadlee?" She doesn't respond, so I knock again and say, "The hospital just called. They've located a liver for my dad. Can you come with me? I need your help."

She swings the door open wide. Her hair's a matted mess, and her mascara has created raccoon eyes that run in black streaks down her face from crying. "They found a donor?"

"Apparently, yes." Searching her eyes, I explain, "The doctor suggested I spend time with him before he goes under anesthesia, just in case it's the last time."

"Okay. Let me get dressed."

I nod. "I'll wait. I can call a Lyft."

"I have parking privileges at the hospital," she yells over her shoulder. "We can take my car."

"Great. Thanks."

I'm pacing in the living room as I wait for her, preparing for the worst. *I'm an only child. Does my dad even have a will?*

Suddenly she appears, seeming refreshed as if she's had ten hours of sleep. She's absolutely beautiful.

She's keeping her distance from me. I get it. I don't like it, but I get it. And I will make my arguments to her after we get through some of this mess.

My motorcycle's in the middle of the driveway, so I push it into her garage before we climb into her SUV to drive to the hospital.

When we arrive, I head right to my dad's room. A nurse is fussing with his IV, and the pain and irritation are evident on his face. Rather than welcome me, he says, "What are you doing here?"

"Your doctor called me. I hear you're having surgery later this morning."

"Yeah, that's what they tell me." He gawks when he sees who's behind me, then lights up. "Hey, Dr. Hadlee. Will you be doing the surgery?"

She comes over and sits on the edge of the bed next to him, taking his hands in hers. "You wouldn't want that. I did a surgery rotation in medical school, but I'm much better at giving shots and checking for ear infections." My dad visibly relaxes as she talks to him, forcing my eyes wide.

"I'd rather get a few shots and be checked for an ear infection," he confides. "Did my asshole son apologize? He doesn't deserve you, you know."

Rather than agree or disagree, she just smiles at him. "Did the doctor walk you through how this will work today?" He nods. I watch on as she translates a complicated surgery, describing what they're going to do so he completely understands. She has him eating out of her hands.

What the fuck am I doing letting this woman go? She knows how fucked up I am, and yet she still wants to be with me.

We sit with my dad until they force us to the surgical waiting room. As they roll him away in his bed, I tell him, "I love you, Dad. Be strong in there."

He yells back, "I love you, too, Cameron. Don't let Hadlee go."

I reach for her hand, and she gives me a reassuring squeeze. As soon as the words are out there, the truth hits me. I care about this woman. She accepts me for me, and I would be a fool to let her go.

I turn to her and bring her in for a bear hug. I nuzzle her neck to whisper in her ear and am caught off-guard by her scent. She's simply intoxicating. "I'm so sorry. I'm just... so... sorry." I find it's all I can say to her at the moment.

"Me, too."

We hold hands as we walk into the waiting room, where all my friends are waiting for us.

Mason stands as soon as he sees me. "How's your dad?"

Everyone moves over to talk to us. The girls try to hug me, but I won't let go of Hadlee's hand. "They just wheeled him into surgery."

"It's an eight-hour surgery," Hadlee explains. "The concern's always rejection."

Emerson has my other hand in hers and says, "Let's go find breakfast. There's a great place near here in Noe Valley."

"Thanks, but I think I'm going to stay here so I'm close if they need me."

She smiles at me. "Well, San Francisco University Hospital Cafeteria, it is."

"Would you like me to get your computer from your house?" Hadlee asks.

I don't want her to go, but she has a job. We all have jobs. They don't need to stay here while I wait. It's going to be the end of the day before we know anything. "You all need to work. I'm okay here alone."

Hadlee squeezes my hand again. "Actually, today's my day off, so I can stay."

"We're here for you, man," Dillon says. "Don't worry. The company isn't going to fall apart if we're working remotely today."

Everyone agrees, and Hadlee leans over and says, "Hey, listen. We're a team now. No matter what happens, I'm here with you. Okay?"

Despite the oppressiveness of being in a surgery waiting room, my heart soars. I leave my cell phone number with the surgical desk, and we head downstairs to the cafeteria. Annabel joins us, talking away with anyone who will talk to her. Dillon rolls his eyes, and I'm comforted knowing I'm not the only one irritated by her. Her relationship with Mason's going to create issues, but I'm not going to worry about that today. I have plenty of other things to occupy my mind at the moment.

The cafeteria's a mix of hospital staff and families. Hadlee makes some recommendations of things we may want to stay away from. "The corned beef hash may be a few days old," she shares, "but the breakfast burritos are outstanding."

Almost all of us order the burrito, and each one's the size of a brick. Filled with chorizo sausage, scrambled eggs, and potatoes and then covered in pork green chili—she's right, it's outstanding. It's so large that she and Emerson split one and they still have still leftovers.

We vacillate between joking and jovial to somber and sad. As I glance around the table, I'm grateful to have so many friends here who care about me.

A man walks up to the table. "Hadlee, good to see you this morning."

She blanches. "Ken."

In a condescending tone, he asks, "Who are these people?"

"Well, Ken, these are my friends. And we're all here to support my boyfriend, Cameron." She motions to me. "His father's in surgery today getting a liver transplant."

"You didn't mention you had a boyfriend last night at dinner."

"It wasn't a date, Ken, it was a business dinner. And if you'd kept your hands to yourself, you might've had company for dinner."

I'm floored when she refers to me as her boyfriend, and then within a few seconds, I see red. I'm ready to take this guy out for touching my girl. I stand up and pull my shoulders back. "Do you have a problem, Ken?"

"N-n-no. She may have set the dinner up to discuss a difficult patient, but she wanted a date."

I growl at him. "Sounds like she *didn't* want a date, and you ate alone." Waving him away, I say, "You can leave now."

Ken appears surprised by my directness but turns quickly and scurries off.

As soon as he's out of hearing distance, Hadlee says to the group, "I'm sorry. Ken was a letch who I met for dinner to discuss a difficult patient we share. His hands kept wandering, and I warned him but he didn't stop, so I left him at the restaurant and came home. Cameron isn't my boyfriend. I just wanted Ken to go away."

I'm not having any of this. "Wait a minute. I *am* your boyfriend. We're working toward something. I'm absolutely your fucking boyfriend." Staring at the group, I state firmly, "Don't even think you can fix her up with any of your friends or people you meet. She's off the market. Permanently."

I'm not sure if the look on her face is one of horror or shock, but the guys all grin at me like I finally get it.

Greer and Emerson jump from the table and rush up to us. "We're so happy for you." They yank her into a group hug.

Annabel jumps up and attempts to join the hug. "I'm so glad there's another one of us who doesn't work for SHN and is part of this crowd. The Sunday night dinners tend to get boring when they go behind closed doors to meet."

Hadlee's all grace when she says, "Wonderful. If I'm invited on a Sunday night, we'll have to find something to occupy ourselves. I grew up next door to the Arnaults, so I know a few things we can do to keep us busy."

I glance at Mason, and he turns ashen. Maybe there's trouble in paradise after all.

I send the team back to the offices after lunch, and Hadlee's kind enough to head over to my condo and pick up my laptop and a change of clothes. She shows me where the doctor's lounge is so I can clean up. It's astonishing how wonderful you feel after a warm shower.

It's after 5:30 p.m. when the doctor comes over to speak to me. "Mr. Newhouse?"

We all stand. "Yes?"

Hadlee takes me by the hand, and he stares at her with recognition but says to me, "Your dad 's currently in a stable condition. He'll be in recovery for another forty-five minutes before we move him to the ICU for about a week. It'll be after visiting hours by that point, so you can go home. We don't expect your dad to wake tonight."

I nod, and Hadlee asks, "Rick, how are his numbers looking?"

He glances at me to make sure I'm okay with her asking questions, and I nod. He then jumps into a highly technical conversation with Hadlee. She turns to me and says, "What all of that means is that his numbers seem good twelve hours post-op and he isn't showing any initial signs of rejection. Over the next few days, we're going to watch to be sure his levels stay in a certain range. The levels will move around a lot as they determine the correct dosage and combination of rejection medications for him."

I'm relieved to have Hadlee here with me.

The doctor grins. "She's awesome, isn't she? She was top of our class. She could've had any residency in any program, and she chose pediatrics here in San Francisco. It's almost a waste of her talent."

"Not true, Rick. You're too kind," she says as she shakes her head and turns a beautiful shade of pink.

"I certainly think she's pretty awesome," I assure him, and we agree to meet tomorrow.

Turning to me, Hadlee says, "Let's get you home."

I thank the team for staying with me. We are all tired and begin walking down to the garage. Greer asks, "Does anyone need a lift?"

"No, thanks. See everyone at the office tomorrow?" Everyone agrees and he turns to me, "Cameron, take whatever time you need."

"Thanks, man."

Pulling out of the parking garage, I joke, "Please tell me we're heading over to my place."

"Yes. When I picked up your computer, I packed an overnight bag."

"Well, I hope you realize we're either going to make your house a rental property, or we can sell it and you can put that money back into your trust fund. It's your choice, but you aren't going back there to live." I may be a bit slow, but I'm not letting her out of my grasp again. I'm crazy about her, and I want it to be clear to her and everyone else. Hadlee and I belong together.

"I don't know," she hedges. "We've only just announced that we're dating to our friends. That's a big leap."

"Hadlee, if you're nervous about me, I get that. *I'm* nervous about me. Maybe making it a rental for a while will make you feel better. And I'm fine if we make my place a rental and find something that's ours, as long as we find a house with a downstairs apartment. I hope you're okay if my dad lives downstairs?"

"You're just moving so fast. A week ago, I was asking to be more than a fun-fuck, and now you're talking about heading down a path that includes forever. I think I have whiplash."

I cringe internally. I hurt her, but I will spend the rest of my life trying to make it up to her. "I didn't realize how important you were to me until you moved out. Then with that jerk Ken in the cafeteria this morning, I wanted to punch him in the face knowing he touched you without your permission. But what did me in was how great you were with my dad. Not only did you get him settled and relaxed before surgery, but also talking to the doctor after surgery. You're simply wonderful, and I want that in my life for the rest of my life."

Her eyes widen and her jaw is slack. I know I took her by surprise, admitting so much after our previous talks, but I'm determined to make this work. She puts her hands on her hips, and I'm prepared for a lecture. "Okay, I'm not sure that you've changed my mind, but let's agree to take it one day at a time. When my house is completely ready, we can discuss next options."

We arrive at my house and bring our things inside. I lead her to my bedroom, and she puts her bag aside and turns to me. Her arms encircle my neck, and she steps in for a long and languid kiss.

"Damn, woman," I breathe heavily when we part. "You're incredible."

"Yeah? Right back at you, handsome. Now shut up and give me what I want."

I dip my tongue back in for another taste, then bite her bottom lip. My nimble fingers make their way under the hem of her T-shirt, and I slowly begin to inch it over her belly as she pushes into me with her desire. When the shirt passes over her glorious breasts, my breath hitches. "God, you're exquisite," I say just above a whisper. She shivers. "I want to see the rest of you," I murmur as I lift her shirt the rest of the way over her head. At the sight of her blue lacey bra, my eyes home in on her incredible breasts. "Blue." I shake my head. "I believe that's my new favorite color."

I pull her back into my body and trail my hands up her flawless back in a slow caress, ending at the clasp of her bra. I unhook it using one hand, and she giggles as her breast are freed. Pulling back, I gaze at her thoughtfully, and she asks, "What?"

I let out a long, low groan. My chest is heaving as I zero in on the delicious pink nipples, my desire to touch, lick, bite, and pull the sweet pink peaks mounting. Hadlee rubs her chest against me, and my breathing becomes rapid with anticipation while I gaze into her eyes with heated lust.

"You're so fucking sexy. Kiss me," I demand.

Unbuttoning her pants, I slip my fingers into her creamy center. Her hips move in a silent request for more. Removing my fingers from her slick core, I lick them slowly. "You taste good, too."

She slips her jeans over her hips, revealing the most glorious pair of see-through blue panties. Slipping my fingers below the elastic band, I plunge into her wet slit once again. I want her more than I've ever wanted anyone.

I back her up to the edge of the bed, and she runs her fingers through my hair, pulling me into a deeper, more frantic kiss. I massage the globes of her ass, pulling her flush with my erection.

Without breaking the kiss, I relish in the softness of her breasts against my hard chest as I lift her onto the bed. I unabashedly explore her breasts with my hands, squeezing and kneading them, pinching and pulling her nipples between my fingers. Laying her flat on the bed, I break the kiss and hover over her body. My breathing labored, her eyes filled with carnal need, I whisper, "I'm going to make you feel so damn good that you won't even remember your name."

Standing, I take my T-shirt off and slip out of my jeans while she watches. Inserting my fingers below the elastic of her panties, I slip them off as she lifts her legs and discards them. "I may hide those again," I tell her with a wink. Spreading her legs open by parting them with my knees, I let out an appreciative moan. She makes me feels so strong and capable.

She trembles as I lick my lips, swallow hard, and whisper, "I want to taste you, Hadlee." I move my gaze from her beautiful clit and rasp, "Can I?"

She nods, and I run my hands up the inside of her creamy

thighs, pushing her legs farther apart and exposing her to the open air. My cock's hard and begging for her touch, but I want her to know I'm in love with her.

"Cameron... please...," she cries out desperately, but I take my sweet time, taunting her, teasing her.

"Don't you know good things come to those who wait?"

chapter THIRTY

CAMERON

It's been an awesome few weeks. My dad was in the ICU for two days, then the main hospital ward for two weeks. He was moved to a care facility attached to the hospital after that and has been there for almost a month. Watching my dad improve daily has been great. Hadlee checks on him each time she visits the hospital and will send me some kind of update: a photo, something he said, or notes about his overall disposition.

Sitting at the breakfast table, watching the morning begin as the mourning doves coo and sing their songs, I'm happier than I've been in a very long time. I reminisce over how much the last year has changed my life. I found a woman who accepts me for me, and I've started to develop a better relationship with my dad. What more could I ask for, honestly?

"Cameron, did you hear what I said?" Hadlee asks as she stares at me across the table.

I look at her. I haven't been listening, and she knows it. Her head tilted to the side, there's a sparkle in her eyes, and she's smiling.

"Well? What do you think? Can we finally do it?"

"I'm sorry. I was thinking about my dad. He should finally be home in the next two weeks, but he thinks the apartment downstairs is too nice for him."

"I told you I wanted to have you tie me up for sex and you're thinking about your dad?"

"Well, yeah. Wait, you said what?"

She lets out the most melodious laugh, her breasts jiggling a bit, and the sight makes me hard. "I'm ready whenever you are," I growl. "Tying you up is about your pleasure. It means you submitting to me while together we both enjoy ourselves."

"Well, you've been teasing me for months, and rather than waiting patiently for you to bring it up, I'm here and begging for it." She bites her lip, and I don't think she realizes how sexy it is.

Reaching across the table, I run my finger up her arm and caress her exposed delicious skin. "Begging? I like when you beg me to finally let you come. You're amazing, you know that?"

She comes over and sits on my lap. "Sweetheart, I know you want this, and I'm ready to explore. I trust you completely."

She's wearing a thin T-shirt, and her breasts are calling to me to be played with. Circling an areola, the nipple beads and I pinch it. Despite the T-shirt and the bra, she's responsive and pushes into my hand. I love what she does to me and how wanton she is. Whispering, I ask, "Are you going out with the girls tonight?"

"No. You can have me all to yourself. What do you think we should do?" She kisses the nape of my neck, nipping and rubbing her nose along the skin, making my dick harder. "I have rounds to do at the hospital this morning, but I should be back by two."

"That would work. Any hard limits?" I eye her carefully. Any hesitation means she would be doing this for me and not for us.

"What are hard limits?"

"Things that are absolutely out of the question."

"Well, I want it to be just the two of us."

I laugh at that. "Don't worry. You're more than enough for me."

"Okay. Well it can't leave any marks, so probably things like silk ties rather than a cotton rope. I don't want to explain to the parents of my patients that I let my boyfriend tie me up and fuck me ten different ways."

"Are you worried they may want to join us?"

Swatting at me playfully, she giggles. "No, silly. I love all the naughty things we do together"—she rubs my cock through my jeans—"but I want our private life to remain private."

"I couldn't agree more." I don't want her to stop, but if we do what she wants later, I'll need all the energy I have to keep up with my little minx. "When you get back from the hospital, we can experiment."

Standing up, she puts both hands on my knees and leans in for a deep and lasting kiss that's both aggressive and wanting. I break away and warn, "If you don't stop, you won't make rounds today. And I have big plans for you."

Straddling me, she looks me straight in the eye. "Promise? I want this with you, Cameron."

"Oh, I promise. I can't wait to make you come over and over again."

She grasps my cock through my jeans and purrs, "I hope you're going to find a few orgasms in there, too."

I swat her on her behind. "Don't worry about me. Just go do your rounds. I'll be ready when you return."

We kiss deeply, and then she grabs her things and heads to the hospital.

While she's gone, I need to get ready and run a few errands. Candles in her favorite lavender scent are on my agenda, plus a stop at the adult store for a few goodies.

I'm nervous and excited. This takes us to a whole new level, though I'm trying not to put too much into it; if she doesn't like it, I really think I'll be able to live without this level of kink in our sex life.

I inhale deeply and then release the air slowly, letting my tension go with it, leaving pure excitement behind. My body feels charged, alive, my muscles rippling with energy. I flex and release my fingers to let some of it go, and when that's not enough, I shake my arms hard.

Yeah, that's better. Phew.

The door slides open and Hadlee steps out of the shower completely naked, her wet hair brushed back from her flushed face, her smooth skin damp. She takes in the transformed ambiance of our bedroom, scanning the candles burning all around us, though my body blocks the bed from view. Her blue gaze lights up before it meets mine and darkens, her obvious desire mirroring my own. The air between us seems to crackle with expectation.

"Come here, sweetheart." My voice is low, thick. She smiles faintly and steps forward as I move back, then stop. She stands right in front of me, hands at her sides, chin up, shoulders back, breathing fast. *She's excited.* Knowing she needs this, wants this, makes my blood boil in urgency. At the same time, the added weight of responsibility centers me, stabilizing me as it settles low in my belly.

Here we go.

With a brief smile, I lift my hands to trail my fingertips lightly along her arms. Goose bumps flare on her skin in response. *So pretty.*

"My beautiful sweetheart." She smiles tentatively. I bend to place a light kiss on her lips. "Ready to play?"

Hadlee nods, and I stare into her eyes. "Words, sweetheart. When we do this, use your words to answer my questions."

"Yes. I'm ready to play."

I smile. "So am I." Taking her hand, I draw her over to the side of the bed. "Let's get you settled, then. Up on the bed, on your back. Cushion under your hips."

She turns to do as told but then hesitates, biting her lip as she looks from the bed to me with a deep frown on her face. "Um...."

I raise an eyebrow questioningly, and she seems torn with some kind of internal debate until finally she blurts out, "I thought I said rope was a hard limit for me?"

My stomach drops a little. *Damn. I should've explained.* Taking her hands in mine, I squeeze them lightly, reassuringly. "What I heard was leaving visible marks was your hard limit." She nods, and I continue. "I found a way to make it work."

She raises her chin, still looking unconvinced. "How?"

"I—" I start, then think again. "Here, let me show you."

Turning her around, I take out one of the ring knots from under the bath towel I laid across the bed, holding it out for her. She grabs it and then looks it over from all directions.

"What am I looking at, exactly?" she asks, her tone still guarded.

I step closer and take the rope from her hands, pulling hard at the ring on one end of the knot and the long tail on the other.

"It's called a ring knot. See? It won't tighten on you, no matter how hard you pull." I tuck my thumb into my palm and wiggle my hand into the ring, then grab the rope above the knot. "Which means you get the sensation of being tied up, but at the same time"—I squeeze my hand out of the ring—"you can simply take your hand out if you need to. Your hands are smaller than mine, so it would be even smoother."

"Oh, I see."

Her voice sounds breezy, as if she'd just released her breath after holding it in for too long. Then she slips her hand into the ring, holds on to the knot, and pulls hard. *That's right, sweetheart. Check for yourself.* She tugs the rope a few more times, then takes her hand out and raises her face to me, her smile growing ever wider with each passing heartbeat.

"So, sweetheart, would you like for me to tie you up and have my naughty way with you?"

She giggles and nods enthusiastically. "Oh yes, please. I would very much!"

I laugh, too, my anxiety melting away at her expectant tone. *God, I love this woman.* I shake my head and take a step closer, cupping her face and kissing her slowly, sweetly.

"Hmm. I'd like that very much, too," I murmur against her soft, pink, pouty lips. After one more quick taste, I step back, needing a little space to gather my wits around me. *For this to be as good as it can be between us, I have a role to play.* I close my eyes and take a moment to regain my equilibrium. When I'm ready, I open them and refocus on Hadlee, who stands naked and expectant in front of me. *I'd better not stall too damn long.*

"On the bed, then, sweetheart. On your back, cushion under your hips."

When she doesn't move immediately, just breathes in and stares at me with a soft smile, I fight my own grin, trying instead for a menacing scowl. "You had a good excuse to hesitate before, sweetheart. Not anymore. If there isn't a *very* good reason for your behavior, young lady, I'd suggest you get your lovely ass on that bed, *now.*"

Her choked "Oh, yes!" sounds suspiciously giggly, but then she turns to climb up on the bed, and the sight of her luscious behind wiggling so close to my face is enough to make me forget anything and everything except the need to bury myself deep inside her.

I clench my fists and strive for composure as Hadlee flips over and settles on top of the thick towel. The pillow forces her back to arch slightly and her pelvis to tilt, pushing her beautiful pussy up high, putting it on display for me. Without being told, she spreads her arms and legs wide and then relaxes into the bed, clearly waiting for me to make the next move.

God, she's perfect.

"Very good, sweetheart. That's more like it. Now let's get you nice and tied, shall we?"

She whimpers in response and my dick surges, even as I move to slip her right hand into the first ring knot. I note with satisfaction that the fit is just right—loose enough for her to easily release herself, but still tight enough to provide the illusion of helplessness—and move on to her legs before finally securing her left wrist. When I'm done, the sight before me—Hadlee naked and bound, spread-eagle by the purple rope, her hips pushed up invitingly, passion plain as day on her face—makes my heart slam hard in my chest.

I grind my teeth. *Focus, Cameron.*

"How's that feel, baby?" My voice sounds hoarse, but I can't help it.

Hadlee tugs at the ropes and a slow smile spreads on her flushed face. "It feels—shit! It feels absolutely amazing. Just... I love it!"

I nod. "I love it, too, sweetheart. You look incredible like that. Gorgeous."

It's an effort to keep my voice calm, and I'm damn proud of myself for succeeding. Moving closer, I lean one knee on the bed next to her torso, caress her face lightly with my fingertips, moving slow and gentle down her throat and along the middle of her beautiful, naked torso. Hadlee's lips part to allow for her quickened breath, curling upward as she watches me watching her.

I don't try to hide my desire for her, and her own eyes darken, her cheeks colored by matching stains of blush. I can read her mind right then. *'I'm sexy and I know it'* is written all over her face, and I love it, love her for owning up to it, for reveling in her own body.

Absolutely fucking *gorgeous.*

I continue the path toward her spread-open pussy but then avoid it, instead moving down one thigh toward her knee while humming my favorite tune. She arches into my touch and then slumps back when I don't go where she wants it. I chuckle and repeat the journey up her body and then down again, moving in a slow, hypnotic rhythm. My touch is light, almost ticklish. I know she wants more, and I thoroughly enjoy denying her.

For now.

"Don't be greedy, sweetheart. Patience is a virtue."

She whimpers at my game, but at the same time, her face softens into beautiful acceptance. I smile approvingly.

"Now, here are the rules. First, while you *can* release yourself any time you choose to, you *may not* do it for any reason other than for your safety. So, if you want to be untied *not* because you feel you're at risk but for any other reason—discomfort, whatever— you need to ask and wait for me to do that for you, okay?"

"Yes," she answers softly.

"Good. Now I'm going to blindfold you in a moment, and although I'm sure you'd be able to remove it even without using your hands, I'd like for you to keep it on, and if need be, ask me to remove it for you."

Her eyes hold mine as she nods solemnly. "Okay."

I can see her questions and doubts rising. For a moment, I consider letting her struggle through them on her own, but I suspect it's too soon. For now, at least, it's my job to help her with them.

I stretch out on my side, my body close to hers but not touching, and cup her smooth cheek as I hold her gaze with mine.

"We need to practice trust, baby," I say quietly. "I need to see you speak up when there's anything wrong, and you need to see me taking care of it—of you—while we have that safety in place in case." I'm relieved that her face clear as she nods slowly.

"Yes, I understand." She bites her lower lip and then rushes, "Do you want me to use any special safe words?"

I consider her question. I know I'd stop at any sign of distress, regardless of safe words, but I'm happy to practice using those, too. “Sure, let's go with the standard traffic lights—red and yellow. All right?”

“I—yes, please.” Her mouth curves slowly upward, and then her lips part to allow her tongue a quick lick across them, almost making me forget my line of thought. I resist the distraction, just barely.

“Okay then. Red and yellow. Don't hesitate to use them, either. This is what practice is all about, okay?”

Her grin widens. “Yes, sir.” Her eyes crinkle at the corners, and then she bites her lip and looks me up and down before catching my gaze with hers. “Um, may I use green, too?”

I tilt my head but nod. “Of course. Green’s good.”

She giggles, then throws her head back and shouts up to the room, “*Green!* Please, please, I’m so fucking green right now!”

I burst out laughing even as I roll over to straddle her hips. As I straighten up and loom tall above her bound, spread form, my amusement quickly dissipates, replaced with thick, hard lust. I’m still fully dressed in my jeans and T-shirt, only my feet bare, while she’s utterly naked below me. I’m bigger and stronger and completely in control, and by God, the sense of power is intoxicating. I stay there, keeping my weight on my knees and my eyes locked with Hadlee's, and breathe it in, letting it wash over me, into me, filling me up until I'm steadfast and centered.

Yes, this is what it’s all about.

I look down at her, then slowly lean over and take her mouth in a slow, hot kiss. She welcomes my lips and my tongue, opening up to me, drawing me in as she arches up to try and rub her naked chest against my torso. I chuckle and pull back, all the way off her and up to my feet next to the bed.

"Oh no, sweetheart, we've only just started. Now, where's that pretty silk scarf of yours?"

I turn to her dresser and find her lingerie drawer, figuring she may keep some other delicates there as well. Soon I find the long scrap of slippery lavender-colored silk—and under it, a real treasure. With a delighted chuckle, I grab it and turn around, waving the realistically shaped, flesh-toned silicone cock between us.

"Well, well, well. What have we here?"

Hadlee blushes beet red and bites her lip, then meets my eyes boldly.

"Umm, Cameron, please meet my very close, loyal, and long-time friend, Dan the Dildo. Dan, please meet Cameron, my boyfriend. I hope you two will play nicely together."

My grin turns feral, exposing my teeth, even while internally I celebrate the title she so easily chose for me. "Tsk, tsk, tsk. Still sassy, even when tied, spread-eagled, and naked? I guess I'll need to do something about that, hmm?"

She breathes a "Yes, sir," as she takes in the unveiled need in my expression. Her cheekiness melts away then, leaving her vulnerable, aroused, and expectant before me.

I take my time absorbing the sight of her. I've never seen her so beautiful. The candlelight flickers along her curves, accentuating their supple smoothness. With her hands tied above her head, her breasts are pushed higher on her chest, the shadows around them forming almost perfect circles while light accentuates their fullness, gleaming over her creamy globes. As my eyes roam her body, her light pink nipples harden under my gaze, pushing out and up, begging to be touched.

Not yet.

My gaze trails lower, watching her midriff ripple with her excitement. Lower still to her softly rounded belly, the darkened dip of her belly button rising and falling rhythmically, hypnotically. I watch it for a few more heartbeats until a gleam of moisture twinkles at me from between her spread thighs, pulling my attention there.

Her hairless pussy with its slit glistening, red-pink and swollen, and her tight opening, already coated with her sweet-smelling and wonderfully tasting juices.

My dick, swollen and ready, tries to push itself out of my jeans, but I ignore it. My need to control Hadlee, to play her body and her mind, to take her places she's never been before is far, far greater than my need to fuck her.

I breathe deep and slow, letting that buzz flow through me, bring every cell in my body alive.

Hadlee whimpers softly and arches her back, her face flushed. I shake my head slightly, admonishing her.

"Shh. Lie still."

She pouts a little but does as she's told. I smile approvingly and finally move closer to kneel on the bed. I place the dildo on her torso, nestled in the valley between her breasts, and then hold her silk scarf in front of me.

"Raise your head, sweetheart."

She does, and I tie the scarf over her eyes, knotting it loosely under her, not wanting any uncomfortable lump to annoy her.

"There, how's that feel?" I ask when I finish arranging the silk folds over her eyes to make sure she's completely blindfolded.

"Oh... feels good. Thank you," she says softly, not a trace of sass in her tone.

God, she submits so beautifully. I smile in awed satisfaction, knowing she can't see me. Out loud, I reply, "Mmm, good. Now, you mentioned that you hoped I'd include Dan in our play, didn't you?"

"Oh, yes. Pretty please." She nods enthusiastically, and I chuckle as I pick up the heavy, flesh-toned toy and start trailing it around her breasts. Hadlee responds by arching up, and I withdraw, denying her contact.

"No. Lie still, remember?"

"Yes." Immediately she relaxes onto the bed. "Sorry."

"Hmm. That was your warning, sweetheart. Next time you do that, there'll be consequences."

She gasps and then smiles. "Yes."

We've played this game before. She'd made me spank her ass over and over again by deliberately and repeatedly breaking my "no moving" rule. This time, however, it's not her ass I'm going to spank. We'll see if she likes that.

I bring the dildo to her smiling mouth, trailing it along her lips. She smiles wider and sticks her tongue out to lick along the silicone shaft, making it glide more easily with each passing. I watch, entranced, as her tongue slides lovingly along the fake cock.

Fuck. So sexy.

Changing angles, I rest the fat head on her stretched-out

tongue and nudge forward. Hadlee takes the hint and opens wide, taking a couple of inches into her mouth before hollowing her cheeks and starting to suck for real.

I swear I can feel her mouth on my dick. I breathe hard, grit my teeth, and fuck her mouth deeper with the toy. I stop abruptly and pull out—mostly because I know I'll explode in my pants if I continue—and then glide the toy down her neck to her breasts before gently rolling its wet tip around one nipple, then the other, painting them with her saliva.

Hadlee strains against the ropes holding her arms as she struggles not to move, and I smile down at her. Though she can't see me, I know she can hear the approval in my voice. "Good girl. Stay still."

I tease her nipples a few more times, then bring the dildo back to her lips for more lubrication. "Suck."

Fucking her mouth slowly again with the toy, I look down at her body. I want to touch her so bad; I know she wants me to touch her, too. Between her thighs, a tiny trickle of moisture seeps down between her ass cheeks.

Not yet.

When I pull the fake dick out of her wet lips and circle her nipple with it this time, she arches up high. "Oh please, please!"

I pull it away from her body only to return sharply a moment later, spanking the underside of her breast with her own dildo.

"Ahh, yessss...."

Hadlee sinks back as if absorbing the impact for a moment, then pushes her breasts up, back off the bed, clearly asking for more.

I chuckle and oblige, spanking her other breast a little harder, watching it jiggle up and down from the impact, then bloom with a light pink stripe to match the one already decorating its twin. I rub my palm across both, then firmly squeeze each in turn. Hadlee sighs, and when I remove my hand, she arches her back high again.

"I take it you're green, sweetheart?"

"Oh yes, I'm green. Please, I'm absolutely green!"

I start raining sweet lashes all over her plentiful mounds. The dildo makes a perfect implement to spank her breasts with—thick and heavy, long enough for me to get a good grip but short enough to keep perfect aim, with just a little give and that soft silicone cover to make sure I don't accidentally bruise her. Time seems to melt away as I focus on delivering her body the treatment it so obviously craves. Hadlee moans and squirms at times, but whenever I take a break, she pushes her chest high again, silently asking for more.

I lean over to take her lips in a soft kiss, to show her it's okay. When I'm about to pull back, Hadlee sighs and opens her mouth, her tongue inviting me in. Unable to ignore her request, I deepen the kiss.

After a few long moments, I finally withdraw, looking down at her poor reddened breasts. "Let's make you feel all green again, shall we?"

She smiles tentatively and nods. Reaching over to her dresser, I fish around until I find her lotion. "Hmm, this should do. Let's see."

I remove the silk tie from her eyes. Taking a generous glob, I rub my hands a bit to spread it evenly between them, then bring my palms to Hadlee's breasts gently. The touch of cool cream against her inflamed skin must feel good, because Hadlee first inhales sharply and then exhales slowly before relaxing into my touch, closing her eyes in blissful surrender.

I glide my slippery hands all around her flushed, swollen breasts, aiming to soothe rather than ignite her passion, but after a few gentle strokes, Hadlee moans. "God, that feels good...."

Smiling, I bend down to blow cool air over her cream-covered skin, chilling it further. Hadlee shudders as her nipples crinkle and tighten right in front of my eyes. Before I make any conscious decision, my fingers close around them, rolling each pink, hard peak between thumbs and forefingers, tweaking and pulling on them lightly.

"Oh my gosh!" Hadlee squeals and arches her back high.

"Tsk, tsk, tsk. How quickly she forgets," I mumble, though I know she can hear me, her eyes widening before my fingers squeeze her nipples hard.

"Arrggghhh!"

Hadlee grunts at the brief pain, but then her face softens when my fingers relax their grip, going back to their light, teasing play, pleasuring her. Her arm muscles flex as she pulls hard at her ropes, fighting her need to move.

"Good girl." I smile and reward her by blowing more cool air onto her skin, then licking and sucking on each nipple in turn. I can feel a fine tremor in her body as she struggles with herself, willing her body to keep still under my touch.

God, I love this. Having her like that, completely at my mercy, submitting to my will.

I suck harder, taking more of her breast into my mouth. Hadlee whimpers, and I know the pleasures now tinged with residual pain as her abused tissues are pulled into play, but I keep going regardless, trusting that she'd use the safe word if need be this time around. I release her breast and catch her disappointed sigh before taking the other into my mouth, making her squeal again.

I want to make her come like that, riding the line of pain and pleasure.

The thought makes me hot. Too hot. I all but tear my T-shirt off my body before throwing it carelessly behind my back. When I find Hadlee's eyes again, they're devouring my body with as much greed as mine are hers.

I smile wickedly. *That's tough, sweetheart. I'm the one who calls the shots here.*

My hand starts the journey down her body while my mouth covers her breast again. I stroke down her soft, quivering belly before moving to squeeze her inner thigh, teasing us both by avoiding her pussy for a few seconds longer. I can feel its damp heat calling me, begging me to claim it. I let Hadlee's breast pop out of my lips momentarily as I prop myself up on one arm, needing to watch my own actions as finally, slowly, I move my hand to her center.

I rub along her smooth lower lips, all the way down to her tight asshole and then back up to her clit before thrusting deeper this time, my middle finger sinking into her slick, open slit, sucked right into her tight tunnel.

We both gasp as I push all the way in, almost losing my head when her inner muscles squeeze around my thick digit. Unwilling to give her any power over me—*not right now*—I pull out to tease around her opening, then focus a few moments on the soft spot above it that I've learned can drive her crazy. Only when I feel her melt under my touch do I move my finger another half inch and start rubbing tight, hard circles over her clit.

Hadlee throws her head back and cries out in pleasure. Bringing my forearm under her stretched shoulder, I fist my fingers in the hair at her nape to keep her arched like that while my mouth goes back to feast on her breasts, half-pleasing, half-tormenting her. At the same time, my fingers continue working her clit, edging her ever closer to her climax.

There's nothing for Hadlee to do now but take every sensation I'm giving her and absorb it in her tied, spread-eagled, immobile body. She struggles a little, though not trying to release herself, more like verifying her bonds are still there, holding her in place. Her hands are fisted around the knots holding her rings in place, and she pulls the ropes down toward her head from time to time, which only serves to stretch her whole body up.

Her legs flex repeatedly but are kept spread wide, her toes curling and uncurling in time to my fingers rubbing her clit. She keeps trying to move her head from side to side, but it only increases my pull on her hair. Hadlee keeps doing it anyway, moaning deeply every time she does. Her eyes are tightly shut, her mouth's open, and her cheeks are flushed red—as is her whole body.

I've never wanted a woman more in my life.

Releasing her breast, I take the other one in my mouth and suck it deep, knowing her abused flesh would protest, but also knowing that, at this point, her pleasure would outweigh the pain—would only deepen it, in fact.

Her breath hitches in her throat as a gush of heat soaks my fingers before she bucks and cries out, "Fuck, fuck, fuck!" She strains into my fingers as if suspended in time for a few long moments while I keep stroking hard and quick. She's so wet that thick drops of her juices splash out from my furious rubbing, dampening her thighs and soaking into the towel below. *Yesss!* I hiss in triumph.

Hadlee shudders and slumps back with another whiny "Oh, fuck...." I slow down, reducing the pressure on her still-throbbing clit, but keep going as long as her body continues to spasm until she finally settles back, her chest still heaving.

I still my fingers and release her hair. She rolls her neck lightly from side to side, a slow smile stretching across her sweaty face. Leaving her pussy, I trail my wet fingers up her body to her face, then rub them gently across her lips. She smiles wider and opens her eyes, holding my gaze as she sucks and licks them clean, enjoying her own taste on my skin if her moans are anything to go by. I let her have her fun for a few moments, then move them more purposefully into her mouth, fucking it with two fingers.

Hadlee's eyes widen slightly and then darken, and she sucks deeper still, bobbing her head back and forth.

"What's your color, sweetheart?" I ask, although I know the answer. I pull my fingers out of her mouth, gliding them along her drenched pussy.

"Oh *fuck*, I'm so green right now."

I smile. "Good." I climb off the bed to stand up, looking down at her. She stares back expectantly. Walking around to the foot of the bed, I carefully release Hadlee's legs from the ropes holding them in place. She seems a little disappointed but doesn't protest, and I nod to her with a little smile.

"Raise your hips, sweetheart."

Hadlee groans deeply when she plants her feet against the bed and pushes her hips up. I pull the cushion out from under her and then cup her cheek, looking into her eyes.

"Sore?"

She bites her lip and answers truthfully. "Just a little. My muscles aren't used to this, I guess."

"Hmm. Let's switch you into a different position, then. Can you turn onto your belly?"

She does, albeit awkwardly, crossing her still-bound wrists above her head in the process.

"Good. Now can you get up on your knees and elbows?"

"Mmhmm" comes her muffled reply before she pushes up to take the position, moaning again as her muscles pull and flex, adjusting to it.

"Good girl." I move up and, seeing her wrists are still crossed, pull her higher on the bed so the ropes relax, allowing her to part her arms and lean them straight from elbow to palm on the bed. The ring knots lie atop the backs of her hands. She could slip her hands out easily at any time, but she hasn't—and even now, she makes no move to do so.

Because she wants this. She wants you to dominate her. She wants to submit to you.

On fire for her now, my movements grow sharp. I grab the cushion and shove it over her arms so she can rest her forehead or cheeks against it. I know I'm going to be rough—there's no way I could go gently now—and I don't want to worry about rope burns to her face.

Stepping back, I finally remove my pants and boxers. My dick springs free and my hand goes to it, giving it a long-overdue pull. *God, I need to fuck her so bad.* Moving onto the bed, I settle on my knees behind Hadlee, my cock resting heavily along the crease of her ass, and she wiggles back against me. My hands come down hard, spanking her sharply on both cheeks at once, and then I grab her hips to keep them from moving.

Hadlee shrieks, then giggles and buries her head in the pillow that covers her arms.

“What part of 'stay still' didn't you understand, sweetheart?” I growl, and she giggles again.

“I’m sorry! I'm trying, but it's *so* hard not to move.”

Her tone—not even a tiny bit contrite—tells me all I need to know. She wants it rough. *She wants me to spank her while I fuck her doggy style, her arms still tied with my rope.*

I fist my dick and control her hips with one hand as I rub my head and shaft along her juicy folds several times, gathering lubrication. She wiggles again and I spank her with several quick, open-palm smacks to each side before I grab her ass, using my thumbs to spread her pussy wide, and then slowly sink my dick all the way in.

Feeling her hot, slick inner folds stretch and slide all around me while watching my shaft disappear inside her body, inch by slow inch, it’s all I can do to breathe deep and hold on to my control.

Then she wiggles her ass at me. Again.

My voice is almost unrecognizable. “You want it rough, sweetheart? You want me to spank your ass while I fuck you?”

"Mmm... yes, please!"

Damn. I should probably teach her a lesson about topping from the bottom. I pick up speed and my spankings start ringing in the quiet candle-lit room even as the thought passes briefly through my lust-filled mind.

Another time. Right now, *this* is what I want, and by God, I'm going to take it.

My speed alternates between wild, mad fucking, slapping my pelvis against her ass, my balls against her swollen lips, and then slow and deliberate, allowing me better aim as I spank her hips and outer thighs, coloring them a pretty pink. Her pussy keeps dripping and clenching around me as she gets close, and I want to keep going until she comes again, but soon I feel my control slip, and I know I won't be slowing down this time.

Leaning forward, I search for Hadlee's right hand under the cushion. When I find it, I tug it down, speaking urgently in her ear. "Take your hand out of the ring, sweetheart. I want you to make yourself come again."

Hadlee's only response is a soft whimper. A moment later, her hand emerges from under the pillow and she takes it into her mouth, wetting her fingers before moving them to her pussy, rubbing between her folds while focusing on her swollen clit.

I lean back on my knees and watch her masturbate for me, spanking her as I do, adding heat and color to every part of her upturned ass. Her movements become more frantic, and I can't keep away for another goddamn second. Taking my thick, throbbing, steel-hard dick in my hand, I place its swollen head at her entrance and then drive myself slowly, fully inside.

"Keep going, sweetheart. I want to feel you come all around me."

Her fingers, which had stilled before, go back to work. Sinking my thumbs into her fleshy bottom, I hold her securely in place while I pull back and then plow in once more, then back and again, growing harder and faster with every stroke until I'm pumping into her so fast that my hips look like a blur of movement.

The pleasure's all-consuming. My eyes are closed tight, and I'm only vaguely aware of Hadlee's muted cry and the gush of liquid heat as her channel squeezes hard, pulsating around me. A familiar tingle rushes down my spine, engulfing my balls and then racing up my shaft to explode in utter bliss deep inside her body, filling her with my cum.

"Oh fuck. Jeez, fuck...."

I'm not sure who utters the words; all I know is my head's spinning with pleasure and my lungs scream for air as I fold over her, trembling, sweat dripping from my face onto her back.

I rub the little droplets into Hadlee's own damp skin. At my light touch, she shudders and lets her knees slide out from under her, slumping onto her belly, legs still spread wide with me kneeling between them. I move over her to lie on my side next to her and rub soothingly up and down her back, then farther down along her spanked ass and hips, taking care over the sensitive spots.

After a while, when she still hasn't moved, I ask gently, "Are you okay, sweetheart?"

She nods with a sleepy "Mmhmm" into the pillow, and I release the breath I hadn't realized I was holding.

"Wait right here," I say quietly, getting up to pad over to the shower. I give myself a ten-second wash, then grab a washcloth, wet it, and return to the bed. Hadlee's still in the same position I left her; I carefully wipe the mess between her spread thighs and then nudge her shoulder.

"Hey, wanna roll over, baby? Or are you comfortable like that?"

"I'm good," she says.

I mumble an "Okay" as I get up to toss the washcloth in the laundry basket, blow all the candles out, and crack the window open to let cool air filter in. Then I walk into the living room to bring the pile of pillows and blankets I'd deposited there back to her bed.

When I return, she's flipped onto her back, her head now resting on the pillow and her left wrist still inside the ring. Something surges inside me at the sight. If I hadn't just come, I'd fuck her again, right now.

Instead, I take my time rearranging the bed and shaking out the fluffy blanket, letting it float down to cover her up to her chin. Finally I crawl into bed and lie on my side next to her, leaning in to give her lips a small kiss and then drawing back to look into her eyes.

"You may release yourself from the rope now, sweetheart."

Hadlee smiles at me. "Thank you," she says sweetly as she slips her hand out of the ring, bringing it up to caress my face softly before pulling me in for another kiss.

When we finally part, our gazes lock.

"Thank you for tonight, Cameron. I—I needed this. I needed you, us, like this."

I nod. "Me, too." Settling onto my back, I pull Hadlee over to rest her head on my shoulder, pressing her soft body along mine. Her hand lies limply on my chest and I pick up her hand to kiss her wrist, her pulse fluttering under my lips. I tuck her hand back right over my heart, hug her close, and kiss the crown of her head.

"I love you, Hadlee," I murmur into her hair.

"I love you, too, Cameron," she mumbles back and gives me a small squeeze.

I nod and fall quiet. Even as she drifts off, I find it hard to fall asleep myself. Tonight was everything I'd hoped it to be. She's my perfect package. I know I need to do something about it, and soon. She wants a bunch of kids, and I want to give her that.

Without conscious thought, I go back to focusing my attention on the cool air flowing in through my nostrils and the warm air that tickles my lips on the way out.

Trust and hope.

With that thought, I close my eyes and let my fatigue claim me.

chapter
THIRTY-ONE

HADLEE

THE CONTRACTOR TELLS ME that he was able to move faster without me living in the house, although I think he actually feared Cameron. My house is finally completed, and it looks beautiful—a large three-story frame house with new, vibrant paint and jigsaw scrollwork around the cornices, standing among the others in various repair after the fire. It still has the gingerbread façade, fanciful and over the top, though in the remodel we added a few features, including a combination of bay windows, turrets, and decorated roof lines. We also made some significant renovations to the downstairs apartment, making the bedroom bigger and the kitchen more functional.

This is the first home I ever bought on my own, and it saddens me I won't be living here. Cameron and I discussed it, and we could've made it work, but it would've required a much more significant renovation to convert the house from what is essentially two flats into one house. Even then, we've talked about a house full of children after we marry, so we'd quickly outgrow it.

The inspector removes a packet from his clipboard and hands it to me. "Okay, ma'am, here's the report on the inspection. Your contractor did an outstanding job. You're free to move back in."

"Thank you." I take the paperwork and walk through the house. The dark-stained oak floors have a beautiful shine, the fireplace in the living room a vibrant centerpiece to the entire home. Walking through each room, I note that the bright light of the kitchen is much more modern than before the fire, yet still has a style of Old World charm. The subway tiles that cover the walls above the white cabinets with marble countertops stretch all the way to the fourteen-foot ceilings. Cabinets on the walls have obstructed glass fronts, and the once small window overlooking the backyard is now a wall of windows, allowing in plenty of natural light.

I wander to the bedroom. It remained untouched by the fire, but in the end, we decided to replace the windows and redesign the large bathroom to add a jetted tub and shower stall.

Tomorrow the stager will come and put furniture in both the upstairs and downstairs flat. They expect it to have over a dozen offers.

I smell Cameron's sandalwood scent before I spot him. He walks up behind me and puts his arms around me, asking, "Are you sure about selling? We could make this a nice rental."

"I know, but I think we could use the money from this house and yours to buy something together."

Turning me to stare at him, he places both hands on my shoulders. "That money will go back into your trust, or you can use it to pursue your stepmother. I can afford our house, whatever you decide to buy. I'll take care of you, Hadlee. Always. I promise. I love you."

My heart always races when he tells me that. My birthday wish did come true.

I put my arms around him, resting my head on his shoulder. "I love you, too. How did I get so lucky to find you?"

I give her a deep kiss. When we break, I hold her close and murmur, "I think I'm the lucky one."

She doesn't say much, just looks at me adoringly.

"Well, my dad is hoping to go out for dinner tonight. Are you up for Italian food?" I ask.

"You're going to make me fat. I'm already struggling with my jeans."

"You look fabulous. And who cares anyway? I love you no matter what size you are."

We walk outside holding hands, and I stop and kiss him deeply. "Thank you."

"You haven't even opened your present yet."

"My present?"

He hands me a large box he had stored on the front seat of his car. "Open it."

Lifting the lid, the smell of leather hits me before I fully understand what I'm seeing. I glance up at Cameron in confusion. "What's this?"

Placing the box on the hood of his car, he excitedly shares, "Well, you did say you wanted some leather."

I lift each item from the box to admire it. The top is a beautiful leather thong; how something made of leather can seem delicate is surprising. I hold the leather lace-up bustier to my chest. The generous leather cups are supported by strong underwires, but I worry they won't hold my huge breasts.

Leaning in, he says, "You can wear those to dinner tonight if you'd like."

Heat rushes to my center, and my nipples pebble beneath my bra. I laugh and bite my lower lip. "I don't think the girls will fit."

"Trust me, it'll fit. It's made just for you." He gives me a wet kiss, his excitement radiating from him like a young boy at Christmas who can't wait for me to finish opening my gift. "Keep going."

I lift leather chaps and a jacket from the box, and he confirms, "These are just for the rides. They go over jeans as more protection for your beautiful legs."

I stop and stare at the final item, a beautiful pair of knee-high stiletto lace-up boots. "I love it!" I exclaim. "I think I'm going to look like one sexy dominatrix on the back of your Harley."

"That's what I'm counting on." He leans in and whispers in my ear, "You should see the toys I bought for us to play with."

Rubbing my breasts against his arm, I purr, "I can't wait."

chapter THIRTY-TWO

CAMERON

As I stare across the room at Hadlee, my cock stirs. She seems so ladylike and easygoing as she laughs with my dad at the table with his new "friend" Gina, a nurse he met on one of his many doctor visits. Over the last few months, their friendship seems to be growing into something more.

I've met Gina a few times. She's a sweet woman who manages my dad and his illness well. His cancer is still a small issue, but the oncologist is happy. Together they're like teenagers—sneaking looks at one another, whispering and giggling.

I'm happy that my dad may have found someone who's good for him. I'm even more ecstatic that he's on the mend and is doing so well. After all these years of hating my dad and blaming him for my mother's death, I'm grateful to have another chance with him.

My dad and Gina hold hands and speak in low voices. It's clear that they're falling in love with each other. I'm good with that.

Before we leave, Gina and Hadlee are in the kitchen putting away a dessert she brought over, and my dad pulls me aside. "Does it bother you that I'm dating Gina?"

"No. Should it?"

"She isn't your mom," he says sheepishly.

"Dad, I miss Mom every single day, but you deserve someone who makes you happy. If Gina makes you happy, then I'm thrilled for you."

"I'm thinking of proposing."

"You just started dating. Are you sure?"

"Without a doubt. No one will ever be able to replace your mom, but she's the only woman I've ever considered marrying since your mom died. I'm old, and I don't want to waste a minute without her."

"Then I suppose you better ask her quick before someone else tries to steal her away."

"Son, you have no idea how much that keeps me up at night."

I laugh. "Don't wait too long."

He glares at me seriously and says, "You shouldn't wait either, or some guy's going to swoop in and steel Hadlee away from you."

"No pressure." I know he's right though. I've been thinking about it. We aren't big, over-the-top kind of people; we're low-key, and I want it to be extra special.

The girls return with a vase full of white tulips that Hadlee places in the center of the room, giving them great prominence. "Well, I guess we should go," she says with a smile.

Checking the app on my phone, I tell everyone, "The Lyft is less than two minutes out." We walk outside and Hadlee turns to me, whispering so only I can hear, "Just so you know, I'm wearing my new thong."

I groan at the thought. "I can't wait to see it."

We head to dinner down in Ghirardelli Square. Hadlee picked McCormick and Kuleto's for the huge menu. "There's something on the menu for everyone," she said. And the views are spectacular as well, each booth set up to see across the wide expanse of windows from the Golden Gate Bridge to Alcatraz.

I love that, despite Hadlee growing up as part of the 1 percent, she can talk to anyone. Gina's telling her all about some Spanish soap opera, and she's enthralled.

"I speak fluent Spanish, and my patients' parents have talked about them, but I've never watched one," she shares.

Gina places her hand on Hadlee's arm. "You should. They taught me Spanish, but I have to tell you, they suck you in and you'll never get out."

Hadlee laughs. "Maybe that isn't a good idea."

"I know you're re a doctor and don't have much free time, but I really like them."

"Then on a day we both have off, you can show me."

That's why I love this woman. She's open to trying new things. She would be the same way with the Queen of England.

"Cameron tells me you're looking at a weekend away," Dad says.

"I have leather chaps, jacket, and boots, so now we can go for a good ride on Cameron's Harley," Hadlee proudly announces.

"Where are thinking about going?" Dad asks me.

I turn to Hadlee. "What about a ride along the coast to Big Sur?"

She nods, her fingers rubbing at my crotch under the table.

Yes, I'm one lucky guy.

"YOU ALL SET?" We were supposed to leave almost an hour ago, but Hadlee's been worrying about my dad and making sure he's going to be comfortable alone. Gina's coming over this evening, and Dad warned me that he plans on proposing tonight. I'll tell Hadlee later. She might be too excited and want to stick around this weekend, and I'm dying to see her in her leathers and have her all to myself.

She's adjusting the leather jacket when she joins me outside. It fits snug and shows off every delicious curve. I walk around her, examining her with a light touch. I want to bend her over my bike and fuck her hard and fast with those boots on.

"I'm ready. This leather's going to be hot." A flush begins at her cheeks. We need to get going or she may faint.

"It may be a little warm right now, but once we're moving along the highway, the constant wind will keep you cool. Plus, I want to make sure we protect those beautiful limbs of yours." She just stares at me. "And you look sexy as hell."

"Good to know one of your fetishes is a dominatrix."

I give her a chaste kiss and whisper, "I've never been dominated, but with you, I'd try anything."

I climb on my Fat Boy and start it, the purr of the engine lowering my stress levels. This is a big weekend. I reach out to help her climb on behind me, relishing her fine legs and arms holding me tight. As I adjust her helmet, I tell her, "It's three hours to Big Sur. If you need to stop to use a restroom or want to stretch your legs, tap me on the shoulder."

"No problem." She looks a little nervous, but she relaxes as we make our way to Highway 1 and on to San Jose. It feels right having her with me on my Harley.

As we drive, the view is spectacular. The environment changes from rolling hills that meet the ocean to steep cliffs that offer spectacular jagged rocks with a multitude of white waves crashing against them. She taps me on the shoulder to stop only twice, once because she needed the bathroom after all the coffee she drank this morning and the other because she wants to take some pictures. She takes pictures of me, and we even pose for our own selfie.

God, she's beautiful.

"We'll have spotty cell coverage as we enter the park, and the Big Sur Lodge proudly does not have any Wi-Fi. Are you ready to go off the grid?"

She cocks her head to the side and gazes at me. "I think I can manage a weekend out of touch with CeCe and the girls."

When we arrive at Big Sur, the forest a dense cacophony of green amidst the towering redwoods, I have a plan. I reserved a two-room cottage with one queen bed located up the hill from the main lodge in a tranquil area surrounded by trees.

"You up for stretching your legs? There are some interesting hikes and a great waterfall not too far from here."

She points to her boots, which have a significant heel. "How about I change into something that will lend itself to a hike?"

"Only if you wear them later with your leather thong and bustier."

She chuckles and agrees, then removes her chaps and boots and puts her sneakers on. When she takes off her coat as she unpacks, the bustier shows some movement in her breasts, and my cock becomes rock hard. There's plenty of time for that later. I have plans for this afternoon.

We walk hand in hand along the banks of the river.

Gazing at her, I come to the realization that she's at home here in the forest, or on the back of my motorcycle, or wearing a lab coat—she fits it everywhere.

I hum my tune, and she grips my hand tighter. One day she'll figure out the song, and she'll know. We come to a clearing overlooking a small river. I wrap my arm around her shoulder and pull her in tight, and she puts her arm around my waist. "You've been wonderful with my dad."

"He's a good guy. I'm glad you've both found a good place in your relationship."

"We have," I whisper, the beauty of our surroundings too overwhelming for more than that.

"Sweetheart, I want you to know that you changed my life at Dillon and Emerson's wedding."

"You were my knight in shining armor that night. I thought I was going to have to sleep on the couch in the lobby."

I turn to stare into her beautiful blue eyes. I could get lost in those beauties forever. "It was my lucky night."

"Mine, too."

I begin to hum the song once again. I may not be the greatest singer, but I'm hoping she figures it out soon.

"What's that song?"

I shrug and grin. I lead her to my favorite spot and sit her next to me on a large rock that overlooks a waterfall. "Before I met you, I didn't think I had any chance at having someone in my life. You were the wake-up call I so desperately needed."

She leans into me, and I take her hand in mine. "Hadlee, I'm far from perfect, but I love you with all my heart. You complement me. I'm hard and you're soft. I'm gruff and you're thoughtful. You've made every day better since we met, and I can't imagine my life without you. I want to have as many kids with you as you want. You mean everything to me. Would you make me the happiest man on earth and marry me?"

She seems surprised, and her eyes tear up. "Cameron, you are my world. Nothing would make me happier. Yes, I'll marry you." She kisses me tenderly, and it only confirms that she's the woman for me.

I remove a beautiful Cartier diamond ring from my pocket and present it to her. "If you don't like this, we can pick something else. I know it's too much for work, but the wedding band we could use was my mothers, and it's much more understated."

Her brow creases as she stares at the ring on her finger. "This is absolutely perfect. I love it," she whispers, then turns to me. "And I love you."

We sit by the falls for a short time before walking back to the cottage. I pull up the song that I've been humming, Lonestar's "Amazed," on my iPhone and hit Play.

She peers at me with surprise and awe. "That's the song you've been humming since we met."

"I've known for a long time that I'm amazed by you, and I don't know how to say it well, but this song nicely sums it up." We slow dance in the living area as I sing to her.

"I love you, Cameron. Forever and always."

"I love you, too. Now I want to finally enjoy my fiancée."

"Hey, did you propose here because we can't call anyone?"

"There's a good possibility that I want to share this with just you for as long as we can."

"Well, I was kind of hoping you'd tie me up, then tie me down."

I laugh. "You're insatiable and I love it." I smack her bottom. "You better meet me in the bedroom." I remove four silk ties, a fingertip vibrator, and her favorite nipple clamps from my overnight bag. "Make sure all you're wearing is your engagement ring and your boots—nothing else."

Thank you !

Thanks for reading *Venture Capitalist: Desire.* I do hope you enjoyed Cameron and Hadlee's story and reading the third book in the Venture Capitalist series. I appreciate your help in spreading the word, including telling a friend. Before you go, it would mean so much to me if you would take a few minutes to write a review and capture how you feel about what you've read so others may find my work. Reviews help readers find books. Please leave a review on your favorite book site.

Don't miss out on New Releases, Exclusive Giveaways and much more!

- Join Ainsley's **newsletter:** www.ainsleystclaire.com
- Like Ainsley St Claire on **Facebook:** https://www.facebook.com/ainsleystclaire/?notif_id=1513620809190446¬if_t=page_admin

- Join Ainsley's **reader group:** www.ainsleystclaire.com

- Follow Ainsley St Claire on **Twitter:** https://twitter.com/AinsleyStClaire

- Follow Ainsley St Claire on **Pinterest:** https://www.pinterest.ca/ainsleystclaire/

- Follow Ainsley St Claire on **Goodreads:** https://www.goodreads.com/author/show/16752271.Ainsley_St_Claire

- Follow Ainsley St Claire on **Reddit:** https://www.ainsleystclaire.com/www.reddit.com/user/ainsleystclaire

- Visit Ainsley's **website** for her current booklist: www.ainsleystclaire.com

I love to hear from you directly, too. Please feel free to **email** me at ainsley@ainsleystclaire.com or check out my **website** www.ainsleystclaire.com for updates.

Other Books
by Ainsley St Claire

If you loved *Venture Capitalist: Desire*, you may enjoy the other sensual, sexy and romantic stories and books she has published.

The Golf Lesson
(An Erotic Short Story)

In a Perfect World

Venture Capitalist:
Forbidden Love

Venture Capitalist:
Promise

About Ainsley

Ainsley St Claire is a contemporary romance author and adventurer on a lifelong mission to craft sultry storylines and steamy love scenes that captivate her readers. To date, she's best known for her debut "naughty Nicholas Sparks" novel entitled In A Perfect World.

An avid reader since the age of four, Ainsley's love of books knew no genre. After reading came her love of writing, fully immersing herself in the colorful, impassioned world of contemporary romance.

Ainsley's passion immediately shifted to a vocation when, during a night of terrible insomnia, her first book came to her. Ultimately, this is what inspired her to take that next big step. The moment she wrote her first story, the rest was history.

Currently, Ainsley is in the midst of writing her Venture Capitalist series.

When she isn't being a bookworm or typing away her next story on her computer, Ainsley enjoys spending quality family time with her loved ones. She's happily married to her amazing soul mate and is a proud mother of two rambunctious boys. She is also a scotch aficionada and lover of good food (especially melt-in-your-mouth, velvety chocolate). Outside of books, family, and food, Ainsley is a professional sports spectator and an equally terrible golfer and tennis player.